Fiestas and Siestas
Miles Apart

Alan Cuthbertson

Book cover Design: Bruce Salender

Note: Although the events, places, and people described in this book are all real, to protect the innocent and others, a few names and details have been changed.

All photographs taken by Alan Cuthbertson

This book is dedicated to the memory of my father,
Sidney Cuthbertson 1928 – 2007
and
to the people of Ventorros De La Laguna.
Also a special thanks to Heather for all her patience and
support.

CONTENTS

1 In the Beginning ……………………………………… 5

2 Decision Made ……………………...……………… 8

3 House Sold ………………...…………………… 20

4 Spain Here We Come …………...……………… 29

5 Andalucia ………………………………………… 37

6 Back to Blighty ………………………………… 48

7 Welcome to Casa Cuthies ……………………… 53

8 In the *Campo* ………………………………… 62

9 What a Boar …………………...………………… 72

10 A Wedding with a Difference ………………… 78

11 Our First Visitor ……………………………… 86

12 In the Summer Time ……………...…………… 97

13 San Juan …………………………………………110

14 The Hunt ………………………………………125

15 It's the Police …………………………………133

16 Together Again …………………………………140

17 An English Fiesta ……………...………………146

18 It's Christmas …………………………………163

19 An Accident Waiting to Happen ………………167

20 The Price You Pay ……………………………171

21 Whole New World ……………………………180

22 All's Well That Ends Well ……………………188

Chapter 1
In the Beginning

I sat in a quiet corner of the 'Dog and Gun' with my friend Dave. It was his local bar and we had arrived with the double intention of celebrating my 18th birthday and to try and disperse the post holiday blues that had started settling in the day before, when we had returned from a camping trip to Eastbourne. It wasn't working.

"Would you like to make a donation?" I looked up from my glass to see an attractive girl, daintily shaking a pint glass containing a few coins. Always the generous one, I delved into my pockets and asked what the worthy cause was.

"My mother is going to try and down a pint in one go."

"Class," I thought tossing a pound into the glass.

30 minutes later and after a few unsubtle chat up lines, Heather, the collector, and I had arranged to see each other again.

In defence of my now mother-in-law Shirley, this was totally out of character and today you would be hard pushed to find a cheaper drinking companion. Shirley can make half a lager last four hours. No, this particular night was a friend's hen party and she was just entering into the spirit, excuse the pun.

Our first date was the following Saturday. A friend of mine worked for a film company as a runner and had invited us over to

Warrington to see a film being made. When we arrived they were filming a large boat being pulled along the canal; in fact, this is all they did all afternoon but it was a nice day, so what the hell? Whilst Heather was speaking to some of the film crew I leaned on a fence and watched the boat being dragged back once again. I was joined by a young man in an American soldier's uniform, obviously one of the cast. We spoke for about half an hour, discussing how it all wasn't as glamorous as most people think. He summed it up by saying, "At least the pay's okay."

Later we were introduced to the director, who invited us to a party that was to be held that same night; apparently it was a tradition when all the filming was finished.

When filming had finished we went back to Leeds, got changed and then went on to Manchester where the party was to be held in one of the city centre hotels. After eventually finding the hotel it took us a little while to convince the receptionist that we had in fact been invited. In the end she resorted to getting a colleague to escort us to the private room and asking the director to vouch for us.

The drinks, being free, were flowing like water, and most of the guests were already beyond merry and heading for oblivion. Toward the end of the night I sat down for a rest and watched a small group of very drunk men on the dance floor, arms around each other and singing as loudly as possible. From amongst them stepped forward the young soldier I'd been speaking to earlier in the day. He turned to face his friends and began to take his clothes off, stopping only when he'd got down to his rather dated Y fronts. To the side of the dance floor I saw the director, arms crossed and shaking his head. "That's cut his career a bit short," I said to Heather, "Shame as well, seemed a nice lad." Shortly after, we said our thanks to our host and drove back to Leeds.

I found out later that the film being made was *Yanks*, and the exhibitionist in the dated Y fronts? Richard Gere.

Perhaps it didn't do his career any harm after all.

Five months later Heather and I were engaged, and within the year we were married. Dave, by the way, (my friend from the 'Dog and Gun'), came out of the closet, announced he was gay and disappeared into the sunset with a Fijian rugby player named

Clive. Apparently he had been so far back in the closet he must have spent most of his adult life in *Narnia*.

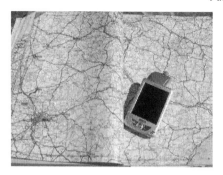

Chapter 2
Decision Made

Twenty-seven years and two daughters later—the daughters being Stacey, 21, and Ashlie, 19—everything came to a head. The office equipment business we had established eighteen years previously was starting to flounder, mainly because we were just bored of being at its beck and call.

The commitment it required meant that for all this time, family holidays for instance, were limited to just two weeks a year. This, for a family that loved travelling, was tantamount to torture. So, when the opportunity to sell the business came, the discussion was short and sweet and the answer unanimous.

At the time the girls had been hinting that they were thinking of going 'travelling' with a group of friends. I knew this would never come off. Although both of them had good jobs and are reasonably good at saving up, and the friends in question were all loyal and sensible, between them they couldn't organise the preverbal piss up in a brewery. I know it's awful to say but my daughters are also the most un-street-wise and naïve individuals you would ever be likely to meet.

Having decided to release the anchor and let the business drift away, we then had to agree on what course should be set for the rest of our lives. "Why don't we move abroad? You and mum have always talked about it." said Stacey excitedly. She was right; the topic had been raised hundreds of times in the past. Ten years ago I had even attended night school for two years studying French. That was until we went to France for the weekend and I found that for some reason I couldn't stand the French. Who was it who said, "France would be a great place if it wasn't for the people"? I returned and changed my course to Spanish, even obtaining a GCSE.

I looked at Stacey and said, "I thought you two were going 'travelling' with the gang?"

"Two of them have backed out already," Stacey replied. "But we are still going; it's just going to be four of us now. Me and Ashlie can come out and join you when we come back." I looked at Heather and found her smiling in some sort of trance. "Are you okay?" I asked.

"Could we actually afford to move abroad?" she asked grinning like a Cheshire cat. "All of us I mean," she added.

For the next few days I was like a man on a mission. My fingers worked the calculator like a concert pianist. One week later I sat the family down to reveal my findings. I dragged out the verdict in true Hitchcock fashion. "With the money we would make on the house, plus our savings, plus the money we got for the business," I looked up from the piece of paper containing my calculations. "And the pensions we have," I looked up again to find them all holding their breath. "We can do it," I announced. Heather, always the practical one, hesitated before joining the girls in the celebration. "What would we do abroad, for a living I mean?"

"Nothing!" was my reply. Then the girls adopted the same curious look that Heather was wearing. "Of course the girls would have to work but we wouldn't," I added.

Over the next few days Heather insisted that I show her a complete breakdown of all the figures. This brought back memories of eighteen years ago when, as a young salesman, I walked in one day and announced that I wanted to set up my own business. At the time she pointed out one or two of the potential problems like we had no money, a large mortgage, two children that were still babies and demanded all of our attention, no experience of running a business, and nowhere to run it from.

"Minor details," I said. But in true Heather fashion she made me do every bit of groundwork and research before she gave the idea her stamp of approval.

I think the only thing we didn't agree on in terms of setting up the business was its name. Heather's choice was 'United Stationers'. Being based in Leeds there was the obvious association with the football team, Leeds United. My suggestion was 'General Stationers', partly because every time you see an advert on television for a stationery product, they always say, "Available from your general stationers." I even had a company slogan:

DON'T PLAY WITH YOUR PRIVATES, DEAL WITH THE GENERAL.

Needless to say we ended up calling the company 'United Stationers'.

After having the house valued and my figures confirmed, the house was put on the market. The ball was rolling. All we had to do then was decide where we would go.

The atlas was brought out and I immediately stamped the table and declared. "You can forget France!"

Throughout the afternoon we gradually eliminated country after country until we were left with Spain. This was due in the main to me discounting every other option raised. There was no way I had studied Spanish for four years at night school to end up in some God forsaken country, not understanding a word they say. In my defence, a few years earlier Heather had also studied Spanish at night school for a couple of years, so I wasn't being totally selfish.

"Spain it is." Everybody around the table sat back, faces beaming with the satisfaction of a job well done. "Don't relax yet," I said. "Spain is a big place. We have to choose where in Spain, for instance the coast or the mountains, the north or the south." Ashlie had by now turned the atlas to the page showing Australia. She elbowed Stacey and prodded the map in front of her. "Don't worry about us," Stacey said with a knowing smirk. "When we come back from travelling you can just let us know where you have ended up."

"Yes, sure Stace," I said with an equally smug grin.

Having been informed by the estate agent that our house may take a while to sell, due of course to the temporary slump in the market place, and not of course due to the fact that for nearly two thousand pounds all they were doing was sticking a postcard sized photo in their window and putting a similar postage stamp sized photo in the local free paper. Heather and I were getting a bit frustrated. "Why don't we get jobs?" I suggested. "It will be a laugh, and it will prevent us from going into our savings. Plus, we are under no pressure so we can choose whatever we want." This foolhardy statement sadly reflects the fact that the last time I had to apply for a job was in the early 1980s. This, to the very young reader, was a time when you could swap and change jobs at will, when the number on the interview panel would quite easily outnumber the applicants.

"But I don't know how to do anything," Heather shot back at me.

"Nonsense," I countered "You have run all the administration for our business for the last eighteen years, books and everything."

"Yes but I have never been on a computer." Unfortunately this was true. During the time our business had grown and developed over nearly two decades, our technology had not. The wholesalers we had used installed a state of the art computer for downloading our orders daily and keeping me in touch with latest offers. Alas, Heather considered the keyboard a machine of the Antichrist and the VDU as Satan's window to our very souls. I may be slightly exaggerating but I think it is safe to say that Heather has never really embraced modern technology. All our paperwork was produced on a typewriter—invoices, credit notes, delivery notes, etc, etc. At times this was slightly embarrassing, especially for a company whose largest area of sales was computer consumables. Then again I suppose I should be grateful that the typewriter was electric. But she did have a point; any job that she applied for would require a degree of computer literacy. Not to be outdone, Heather found a course advertised at our local Adult Education Centre for those new to the computer.

The following week she attended her first lesson. Two hours later I was standing at the door like a mother waiting for the return of her first born on her first school day.

As she strolled down the drive, I asked "Well how did it go, did you learn much?" Looking at her face I think I knew what answer was coming.

"All we did was to learn how to switch it on and type our names and addresses." She lowered herself onto the sofa. "It wasn't the switching on and off that took so long, they are all geriatrics and couldn't find the correct letters on the keyboard to type their addresses." Although Heather didn't know much about computers, she was a damn fast typist. After doing her name and address in about five seconds, she spent the rest of the time going around the class helping the teacher to show the others where the correct keys were.

Between attending the computer classes we sat looking through the local papers picking out jobs for each other. I put my foot down and refused to apply for the strip-o-gram vacancy, especially as it required a 'roly-poly' person. Heather also refused the suggestion I made of applying for the vacancy of sales director for IBM.

"I'm over-qualified," she protested.

I pulled the paper taut between my fingers and sat upright. "There is one for you here."

"What, is NASA looking for a technical assistant?" she joked.

"No, seriously, you once said that you'd always wanted to work in a doctor's surgery. There is an opening here for a medical secretary, no experience necessary, all training given to the successful applicant."

"I suppose I could give it a shot," she said reluctantly.

Stacey was the first home from work that day. She came through the door waving a newspaper cutting. "Look what I have found. It's just what you need." I scanned the top of the slip of paper.

Thinking of moving abroad?

Phrases like: Selling up? Looking for a new start? jumped out at me, so I sat down and read it more carefully. A company called 'Freeform Productions' wanted to hear from people who fitted the above criteria. On went the computer and with Stacey and Heather prompting my answers, I started filling in a questionnaire on their web site.

Later whilst checking my e-mails I noticed a reply from the company whose questionnaire we had filled in. The company in question found members of the general public to go on the popular television show, '*A Place in the Sun*'. They had attached a more detailed questionnaire asking us to define the areas we were interested in, how much we wanted to spend, what kind of property we wanted, and even how we intended to finance the purchase. We answered all their questions, and the last one was "What do you hope to get out of being on the show?" I typed simply, "A NEW LIFE!!"

We were contacted by telephone, not by e-mail. A young researcher told us that they were interested in including Heather and I on one of the shows and asked if we would be willing to go down to London for a short interview and a screen test. "How exciting. Will you be sending us the rail tickets?" The researcher hesitated then added, "Err, no you have to pay the fare."

"Oh, OK. When and where?" After getting the details I hung up and checked the price for a pair of tickets from Leeds to London. Over £100 pounds each for a return ticket!

We arrived at Leeds station and were pleasantly surprised when the train pulled in right on time. Settling into our seats, I looked up to find a smartly dressed couple in the seats facing ours. "London?" I asked our companions.

"Yes." They looked excitedly at each other and then the man added, "We are going to pick up a prize. I won this year's Booker Prize." I can't deny I was impressed. I decided now was not the time to start boasting about our forthcoming screen test.

"That's quite something." I was contemplating asking for his autograph when he said, "In fact we won it last year as well. We ended up going around America as part of the prize." I couldn't believe I was sitting opposite somebody who had won The Booker Prize twice in a row.

"Oh yes, when it comes to selling, I'm your man." His comment confused me a little.

Thirty minutes later the couple opposite had explained how, for two years running they had won the Booker's annual prize. Apparently, 'Booker' is a national catering wholesaler. I don't think I'll bother asking for his autograph.

In London we purchased a street map and located our destination. As we wandered through the East end of London it reminded me of stories told to me by my mother, who was born there in 1934. The German air force had deposited everything it could during the blitz of 1942. When it started to get dark, my mother's job—and remember, she was only 8 years old—was to go and save a spot in the local subway station for the rest of her family. That is where they spent many a night, not knowing if they were going to have a house in the morning or a pile of rubble.

She was, like most children, eventually evacuated. In fact it was during a conversation only 6 months ago that I asked her where she had been sent. "Havatasuck in Wales," She had replied. At the time I recall hesitating before asking if I had heard her correctly. "Just a minute. You're telling me that, at the age of 8, you were sent to Wales, to a place called… Havatasuck?"

"Yes." She answered nonchalantly, and that is where I left the conversation, that is, until during a discussion with a Welsh friend I asked her if there was such a place. "It's actually spelt Abertysswg and pronounced a little differently," she explained.

"Phew! That's a relief," I said.

After a few wrong turns and asking directions from passers-by, we arrived at the offices of Freeform Productions. Entering, we found ourselves in an open plan office with about a dozen people scattered around. They were all on telephones and the accents of different languages floated around the room. On the walls were photographs of people who had previously been selected for the show, and beneath them, charts showing the progress of potential properties and shooting schedules.

We introduced ourselves to the receptionist, who offered us a drink, which we declined, and asked us to take a seat. Within 5 minutes the young researcher I'd spoken to on the phone came around the corner, all enthusiasm and smiles. She showed us into an office behind the receptionist, offered us another drink, and asked us to take a seat. Whilst doing this she was fiddling around with a small video camera on an oversized tripod. "Don't worry about this; it will be working in the background. You'll soon forget about it." She brought the chair from behind a desk and placed it next to ours. "Now tell me all about yourselves."

"Starting from when?" I asked.

"Tell me how you met, where you live, about your hobbies, family, everything."

We spent the next hour going through our life history, always aware that the camera was whirling away, recording everything in the background. "I must point out that if you get selected it will be no holiday. You will be flown out with the crew and be there for about four or five days. During that time you will be up at 6am each morning. You will be taken around to see several houses that our agents over in Spain have narrowed down as being some of the best buys. No meals or drinks will be provided, maybe the odd lunch but that is all. When you look around the properties you will need to go in and out of every room several times, for different camera shots, etc." Heather and I looked at each other and agreed that if it helped us find the house of our dreams then it wouldn't be such a hardship.

"Well I think that's just about everything. I'll go and get the producer. She just needs a quick word." She then winked. "But I can't see any problems." She pushed her chair back, left the room, and closed the door. I nudged Heather, lifted one eyebrow, and tilted my head toward the camera. It may just be my suspicious nature, but I couldn't help thinking we were being watched.

Within minutes, in strode a tall, masculine woman I presumed to be the producer, closely followed by the researcher. A large map was spread across the table and smoothed flat. Southern Spain was just an arms length away. The producer introduced herself, leaned forward and ran her index finger along the coastline just north of Gibraltar. "So this is where we are looking at?" Heather's, mine, and the researcher's heads all lifted at the same time. We all looked at each other in silence. For the last 20 minutes we had been discussing the area just west of Granada, about 50 miles inland from the coast. "No" I said, and then pointed to the area we had been looking at. "This is where we want to view."

The producer lifted her head from the map. "No, no, no, no, no," she replied and then looked across at the researcher. "No, we have a couple for the inland show. It's someone for the coast we need now." Then she walked out of the office. The researcher apologized and said she must have been given the wrong brief. "So what happens now?" I asked.

"Nothing. I am sorry I wasted your time." A minute later we were out on the street and heading back to the railway station. "Not the best £200 we have ever invested, Heather," I muttered, referring to the rail fare we had had to pay.

"At least we met the Booker Prize winner," she said with a smile.

Within three weeks Heather had applied for the job as medical secretary and had been successful. This felt like a challenge; I had to find something. I applied for about ten different jobs and was beginning to feel quite despondent as the majority of them didn't even acknowledge my application. I thought I may have been saved when the estate agent sent somebody over to look at the house, this could mean that we would be off to our new lives without messing around with jobs here in the UK.

When the woman came, the first thing she said was "How many bedrooms does it have?"

"Three," I replied.

"I really wanted four," she said, glancing around and turning her nose up.

That night Heather came home from work full of the cheers of spring. "How did the viewing go?" she asked.

"Not interested," I said over the top of the newspaper. "Just a minute, I've found it," I said prodding the centre of the paper's job section. "Just the thing. A Detention Officer with the West Yorkshire Police."

"They won't have you, you're too old." That had the same effect as slapping me across the face with a gauntlet.

"We'll see about that."

I can't deny that my mind did flash back to the early 1980s. At the time I was a young photocopier salesman, quite disillusioned with the job. After a great deal of thought I decided on a career change and applied to the police.

The entrance exams were to be held at the police headquarters in the centre of Leeds. Rather than book the morning off work as a holiday, I loaded a large photocopier into the back of my company estate car, threw a blanket over it and told my boss I had an appointment with a potential client.

I parked outside the police station and went inside. Before I knew it I had been weighed and measured and sat behind a desk doing an English test.

The alarm bells made everybody jump. The door to the makeshift classroom flew open and a senior officer put his head in and shouted. "Get them out! It's not a drill!"

We were all filed outside where the whole street was in turmoil. Not only had the entire police headquarters been evacuated but the British Telecom building and the neighbouring swimming pool had been emptied as well. (I mean the people, not the water.) Word was passed down the line that it was a car bomb.

I froze.

Making my way to the front of our line, I tugged the sleeve of the officer who had been overseeing our exams. "I think this may be my fault." He stopped, turned and said, "Explain!"

After describing how I had left my car parked at the front of the station, I then went on to mention the blanket covering the machine in the back. I had also had a bump in my car, so I was using the pool car that had been sent over after the Ireland offices closed. I pointed out that the Irish plates and Belfast tax disc may have added to the suspicious appearance.

I was physically dragged to where my car was parked so I could explain the situation to the people who looked like they were about to stack sandbags around my vehicle. When entering the building, the system was to register your car registration and name in a book. Then, every so often, a parking warden comes along, takes all the numbers down of the cars in the car park, and then checks them against the book. Nobody had mentioned any of this to me on my arrival.

After a prolonged bollocking I joined the crowds returning to their previous posts. I continued taking the exams but must admit that I was slightly put off by the others who kept turning in my direction and sniggering. It kept going through my mind that we were currently within a mile of both Yorkshire Television and The Yorkshire Post. This fiasco had to be mentioned.

I left the building by a back door and that night watched both the local and national news with one eye closed. Not a mention. I can only assume that the police didn't want to give the IRA any additional coverage than they were already getting back then.

I was told by post that I hadn't been successful. The explanation was my poor results in the math exam, but I wasn't completely convinced. Surely they wouldn't have kept this all on record anywhere. Would they? I decided to apply for the job as Detention officer, regardless.

Three and a half weeks later I had successfully completed two interviews and a medical examination, without one mention of my previous terrorist exploits. I can't deny that I did feel a little guilty about taking on the job knowing I didn't intend to stay for too long, especially when I found out there was a six-week training course.

The position of detention officer involved working in the cell area of a police station. This was a job historically performed by a police constable but the government of the day thought they would be more productive out on the streets. The training involved everything from first aid and preparing meals, right through to prisoner handling and self-defence. I suppose my warning antenna should have started twitching at this time but along with the rest of the trainees I took it in my stride. We were then shown how to search prisoners, including strip searches, and shown some of the things previously found during these close inspections. The razor blade found inside a young man's cheek was interesting; apparently he had cut a special flap to hold it. The belt buckle that was capable of firing .22 bullets was also slightly worrying.

As the array of weapons began to fill the table, my warning antenna had suddenly began to twitch and the phrase 'what the hell am I doing here?' crossed my mind. As if the point hadn't quite been made, we spent the afternoon looking at full-colour, high gloss photographs of injuries sustained by officers on duty—you know, like the typical Stanley knife down the face or the hammer injury to the back of the head. Along with these were photos of injuries prisoners had given themselves, slashed wrists, a photo of a young girl who had tried to gouge out her own throat, etc. Every single photograph was in full colour and was taken before any medical attention had been administered.

"Any questions?" asked the sergeant instructor.

"Yes," I half raised my hand, "why doesn't anybody call the ambulance before they call the photographer?" My colleagues found this highly amusing; the sad thing was that it was a serious question.

As part of my duties I would be required to take fingerprints, photograph prisoners, and carry out drug tests. Whilst undergoing the training for drug testing we had to obtain saliva from the subject and add it to other chemicals. This would detect opium based drugs and one or two others. I was chosen as the subject to show the demonstration. Everything went well until the result was shown: POSITIVE.

The Inspector doing the demonstration looked as embarrassed as I felt, but not quite as red. He invited me to his office where everything became clear. Apparently I had taken a pain killer that morning for an injury I'd received during 'prisoner handling' training. The drug test had picked up on the codeine the tablet contained. I was allowed to rejoin my class.

When all the training had finished and I reported for duty at the allocated police station, I was introduced to my new boss, the custody sergeant. This man was huge, well over six feet tall and shoulders nearly as wide. At least if there is any trouble I'll be grateful that he's on my side.

I was then introduced to my colleague, the person who would be sharing my duties. I have never met such an arrogant person in all my life. At 25 she, yes she, was a slip of a thing, weighing about 120lbs and full of attitude. If any violence came my way I knew who I would be shouting for back up from, the beefcake with the stripes on his arm.

I could fill the rest of this book detailing the strange events, the weirdos and the oddities that I encountered whilst with the police—but that's not what it's intended to be about. Suffice it to say there is a complete world out there that we 'normal' citizens are protected from. For instance, there was the twelve-year-old boy who raped his younger brother; people who were so drugged up that they bashed their heads into the wall, caving in their own skulls; parents who refused to collect their ten-year-old daughter who was arrested for shoplifting because they were watching *Coronation Street*; to individuals who, when arrested, had to be watched by an officer every minute for fear of suicide—the latter we averaged between 5 and 10 a day.

Chapter 3
House Sold

After another ten months we received a call from the estate agents. It was a Saturday and they had somebody interested in looking at the house the following day. I gathered this was because we had reduced it by £20,000.

We spent the day cleaning the house from top to bottom. Over the previous months our enthusiasm had faded along with the two friends that were supposed to be accompanying Stacey and Ashlie on the big 'travelling adventure'. "We'll just go on our own," they protested.

Sunday morning, as the time of the viewing approached, I actually felt quite nervous. We dashed around the house and made small adjustments to ornaments. Moving a plant pot here, tilting a picture there, making sure everything looked as presentable as possible.

The doorbell chimed.

I'm not sure what I was expecting but had it been nearer to Christmas I would have thought that the two individuals standing in front of me were carol singers. They didn't look old enough to play the lottery let alone have the financial backing to buy a house at close to a quarter of a million pounds.

The young man stepped in, shook my hand and introduced himself and his girlfriend. I presumed she was only his girlfriend because they were too young to get married. My heart sank; Spain looked as far away as ever.

I went through the motions and showed them around the house, if nothing else it was practice for me. They both followed me in and out of every room without saying a word. Probably due to my cynicism since I had been introduced to the inhabitants of the underworld through work, it crossed my mind that they may be just casing the joint. (God, I'm even starting to talk like them).

Back at the front door I asked, "Any questions, anything you would like to see again?" The young man, who I later found out was twenty-two years old, looked at his watch and said. "No, I just popped out during halftime; I will have to get back." He walked out and I slammed the door behind him. "Time wasting tosser," I said to Heather, who looked as disappointed as me. "Well at least the house looks nice now," she said, trying to make a joke out of it.

The doorbell rang and I could see the silhouette of our two young visitors through the glass section of the door. I opened it up and said with more than a hint of sarcasm, "Come back to make me an offer?"

The young man smiled. "Can't stop as I said, but just thought I'd let you know I am going to call in to the estate agents first thing in the morning. We'll take it and I'll give you the full price. Bye." And off he went. I must have been standing at the door with my mouth open for a full minute.

I turned to find Heather had heard the short conversation and looked as shell shocked as me, her eyes glassed over. I closed the door, slowly lifted my jaw off the floor, and what started as a small grin developed into the biggest smile you have ever seen. I jumped clear in the air, clicked my heels to one side, and started singing. "We are off to sunny Spain, a viva España."

A telephone call from the estate agent confirmed that an offer for the full price had been made. Apparently the young man was a computer whiz kid with his own business. He and his girlfriend lived just down the road in a one up, one down, but didn't intend to sell that house, they would just rent it out, and so there was no delay. The estate agent suggested that without a hitch everything should go through within a month.

Stacey walked into the room and announced, "Mine and Ashlie's work visas have arrived in the post."

"What work visas?" I asked.

"For Australia," she replied

"I didn't think you were serious, especially when all your friends had dropped out. I mean you two on your own, what about Spain?"

"Like we said, you and mum go and get somewhere sorted and we will come out next year."

I was dumbstruck. I just could not imagine those two looking after themselves for a full year, living out of a glorified duffle bag. "What will you do for money?" I asked.

"We have been saving up and that's what the visas are for. We will pick up work out there." I looked across at Heather and she shrugged her shoulders. Although they were both grown up, they were, as I said, not street wise and were naive to the extreme. So, not only did we have only one month to sort out everything for Spain, we also had to help the girls with their preparations.

Like everybody, our family had amassed a considerable amount of junk over the years. We weighed up the cost of transporting furniture, etc, but came to the conclusion that we would drive to our new life in the family car and if it didn't fit in the car, then it had to be either sold or given away, whatever it was. I spoke to the young entrepreneur buying our house and he agreed to buy the majority of our furniture.

"What about a car boot sale for the rest?" I suggested to Heather. The frown told me I was going to be on my own on this one. After speaking to a friend, he suggested a regular one held every Sunday next to the Leeds/Bradford airport. "You have to be there at about 5am." He said, "Otherwise you'll get a crap spot and you will be wasting your time."

As well as the family junk, I still had quite a bit of stationery in boxes left over from the family business. Ashlie volunteered her services with the pricing up of everything and even agreed to come with me the following day.

At 4.30am, I think Ashlie was already regretting the offer. We'd loaded the car the previous night, so after a quick coffee we were in the car and off. Even though it was September it was damn cold at that time in the morning.

To my amazement we arrived at the site to find that at least fifty cars had already arrived and were set up. We paid our £5 at the gate and were ushered to the end of the line of vehicles. As soon as I switched off my engine we were surrounded. It was like being on the set of the film *The Living Dead*. About twenty people poked their faces up against the windows of the car. Fortunately my friend had warned me about this. These were the professionals, people who get there first thing, and as sellers arrive, they dive into their wares, hoping to snatch a bargain that they can sell at their own stalls at a much larger price. My friend said that they can recognise the cars of the regulars and when a novice (such as I) turns up, they are classed as easy pickings.

Once we'd lost our novelty and the sun had decided to join the party, the general public started to turn up. I'm not sure what I expected but what surprised me initially was that hardly anybody spoke English. There were Asians, Africans, Eastern Europeans, and people from all over. I am sure that many had been sent by language schools to practice their numbers. Most would point to almost everything on the stall and ask, "How much? How much? How much?" Without any intention to buy.

During a lull I left Ashlie in charge and had a wander around the other stalls. No wonder we were doing reasonably well. The quality of merchandise on some stalls was appalling—just rubbish. If they sold everything on them I think they would struggle to make the £5 entrance fee.

At the end of the day we had disposed of most of what we had brought and made about £150.

A lot of what was left about the house was gathered together and taken to the local charity shop, but we still had some quite bulky things like a 32" television, four push bikes, and a large exercise machine. The police use a local auction house to dispose of unclaimed lost property and recovered goods, so a quick phone call and two days later a van came for everything else we had, except for the television—I sold that to a friend. Unfortunately, as we carried it out to the car we dropped it, so we picked up the bits and delivered them to the local tip.

Heather went with the girls and booked the tickets to Australia and New Zealand via Bangkok. On their return I looked at the tickets, held up the one to Bangkok and said to Heather, "I hope they realise this is a destination and not an instruction." She didn't smile.

Lying in bed that night, I wondered what life had in store for us all. Heather turned to me and said, "Ashlie's not home yet and it's half past one, she told me she was only going to the pub." Stacey hadn't bothered going, she was fast asleep. We don't normally worry about what time they get in at night but Ashlie had said she would be home early to save money on a taxi. "You won't be able to worry about them like this every night while they are away."

Just to put Heather's mind to rest and so I could get some sleep I texted Ashlie, asking, "ALL OK?"

A text came immediately back: "ON WAY HOME BE THERE IN ABOUT 45 MINS X ASH."

We started to settle down but straightaway we heard the floorboards creak in the hall. I sat up and Heather asked, "What was that?"

I whispered back, "Can't be Ashlie, she just said she would be about 45 minutes, plus I never heard the door open." Whenever Ashlie came back from a night out she had the habit of waking the whole house up, fumbling with keys and falling over things.

Creak.

"There it was again," Heather said nervously. Now I've never been a hero but after dealing with scum all day at work the last thing I wanted was one in my house. I slid out of bed and tiptoed across the landing. The man at the bottom of the steps saw me at exactly the same moment that I saw him. I ran down the stairs and he ran away from the door and into the living room. I then realised he must have got in through the conservatory and intended getting out the same way. I thought I'd try and cut him off as he ran around the outside of the house.

Changing direction, I tripped over somebody's shoes and went arse over tit. I was laid there, legs in the air with only my boxers on. Trying to compose myself, I jumped up and went to the door to unlock and unbolt it. Stacey must have woken up and realised what was happening. She shouted down. "He's outside, dad, trying all the cars with your remote!" I shot out into the street just as he had found my car, got in and was driving off. At the end of the street, he slowed the car down, picked up his accomplice and was gone into the night.

Less than one hour later the inside of our house looked like it was hosting my work's Christmas party. Ashlie strolled in slightly the worse for drink and went straight to bed; she didn't even realise anything had happened. "Good night," she shouted as she fell up the stairs. Thank God she didn't bump into our visitors an hour earlier.

My car was recovered a week later without a scratch on it. That was until the fingerprint guys got hold of it with their silver dust. The stuff was everywhere and almost impossible to get off. The only other things taken from the house were my laptop and a digital camera. Both were replaced with insurance and the laptop was due for renewal anyway.

After quite a few nights on the Internet, yes—Heather as well, we had narrowed down our search to the Andalucia area of southern Spain and even contacted a local estate agent with a view to arranging to look at some of their properties. The fact that two years previously we had been on a tour of the area helped us to choose it as a favourable place to settle down.

Stacey sidled up to me and said, "I don't think I am going to have as much money as I thought for travelling. So I am thinking it might be a good idea to not stay in a hotel in Bangkok, but to save our money and sleep on the beach."

"Oh my God we'll never see them again," I said under my breath.

The day came when we were to take the girls to the airport. We went out to lunch and brought along Ashlie's boyfriend, Scott, to say his goodbyes. His eyes filled up more than once but he blamed this on the football injury he received two days earlier. In his defence, he was on crutches. He had also intended to go and join them for a spell in the New Year but because of the injury this was now in doubt. I was as disappointed as he was. Having him travel with them, even for a short while, may have made me feel a little more relaxed.

I felt like just giving the girls a warning about who they speak to, where they go, and not to carry bags for other people, especially at the airport, would have gone in one ear and out the other. So during the weeks leading up to their departure I offered to take them to the pictures.

The film we went to see was *Wolf Creek*. The film showed two girls, travelling around Australia, who then accept a lift from a stranger in the outback. As the film progresses the girls are taken to the man's hideaway. This consisted of a corrugated shed surrounded by rusty cars and chained dogs. They were then subjected to unspeakable torture, and one of the girls dies. All good, family fun. As we left the cinema, both Stacey and Ashlie agreed that there would be no way they would be setting foot in the outback or accepting a lift from a stranger.

The next night we all sat around the television at home and watched the true story of a girl getting beaten and abused in a Bangkok prison. Unbeknownst to her, her new boyfriend had bought her a cuddly toy that contained cocaine, a fact that only came to light at the Bangkok airport.

"Anybody buys me anything over there, I'm binning it" said Stacey

"Me too," agreed Ashlie.

A job well done I think.

The farewell was slightly tearful with everybody making fun of the situation and putting a brave face on. They were flying from Manchester to Heathrow then on to Bangkok, and the connection flight was due to leave only thirty minutes after they touched down. It was going to be a close call.

I gave them one last hug and asked them to text me to confirm they had made the connection at Heathrow. Stacey tutted, "It will be okay dad, stop worrying." They waddled off under the vast weight of their rucksacks that even today I am convinced were full of hairdryers, straighteners, and make up.

Fifteen minutes later I received a text from Ashlie. Stacey had been stopped and questioned. They thought she looked under sixteen years old and too young to travel on her own. Two hours later I received another text. They had been asked to provide proof of age when ordering a drink on the plane.

That night I awoke to the sound of my mobile telling me I had received a text message. It said that they had arrived in Bangkok but their bags hadn't, they had been promised for the next day. Having been given some compensation, £30 each for toiletries, etc. Ashlie informed me that she wasn't going to waste it on soap, they were going straight out for a "good old session" as she put it.

Five days before we were due to set off for Spain I had a phone call from my sister; my father had been rushed into hospital. I arrived at the Leeds General Infirmary within the hour to find my mother crying in the reception area. Apparently my father had had a massive stroke and was quite ill. We went to his cubical where my sister was sitting with him.

My father is seventy-seven years old and to be truthful he had suffered with various illnesses throughout his life. The year before, he had survived a very bad case of pneumonia. A quiet man who said little but possessed a sharp sense of humour and never swore was transformed when admitted to hospital. This was something we noticed many years ago and we called it his "hospital Tourettes." He would lie there 'f-ing' and blinding for England.

It appeared he didn't recognise anybody or remember anything. A doctor came in with a pad and asked us a series of questions regarding his general health. She then said she was going to give him a memory test.

"Sidney," she called, getting his attention. "When did the first world war start?" His face was blank. "Who was Prime Minister during the second world war?" Blank. "Sidney, when was the Queen crowned?" Blank. It was then that I noticed that my mother, sister and I were all wearing the same blank looks as my father. The doctor jotted something down and left. We all looked up and burst out laughing. Every one of us was wondering if maybe we should be admitted as well. If nothing else this helped break the tension we all felt.

Eighteen hours later a bed was at last found for him on a ward. His speech was distorted and confused but he had not suffered the paralysis that often accompanies a stroke.

I visited my father every day that week and each day he had improved, some days only very slightly. Riddled with the guilt of my forthcoming departure, I offered to delay our move and was fully supported by Heather, but my mother wouldn't hear of it.

The day finally arrived when the car was to be loaded and the rest of the Cuthbertson household left for new pastures, except for Digby and Ollie, the family cats that were to stay with Heather's sister, Pamela, until we were settled. It was arranged that we would call in to see my mother and then go to the hospital before starting our journey.

I had calculated precisely the capacity of the car and therefore I was confident that the pile of things that now filled our hallway would fit exactly into the empty estate car parked outside. The neighbours that came over the night before to say their goodbyes were taking bets as to how much we would have to leave behind. But when loaded, everything fit in....just barely.

As agreed we called in to see my mother and spent a couple of hours talking about old times. We kissed and said our goodbyes. I promised to come back in three months to see how everybody was getting on, and I also made her promise to call me if my father's condition deteriorated. "I'll be on the next flight back," I insisted.

I decided to go by the hospital to say goodbye to my father, acutely aware that it could well be the last time I would see him. Pulling up outside, Heather tactfully offered to wait in the car. "I'll only be a couple of minutes," I said, leaving her and the car double-parked. I walked into the ward to find my father sitting on the side of the bed trying in vain to feed himself. I watched him from a distance for a few minutes and considered how cruel fate can be, his hand shaking so much most of the food had dropped from the spoon before reaching his mouth. Stepping forward I announced my presence. "Hi dad, how are you today?" He looked up, frowning, obviously searching his memory to put a name to the face. "Oh fine, fine," He replied, putting down his spoon. "Just thought I'd pop in and say cheerio."

He frowned once again. "Oh yes you're going, aw...." The end of the sentence was drowned in a sea of jumbled words. He stopped trying as frustration got the better of him.

"I won't be far away," I said, "just a couple of hours by plane."

He had never been a man to show his feelings. I felt like this was the one time he actually wanted to say something from the heart. "Look after yourself," he stammered, and then held out both arms. For the first time I can ever remember we embraced. As we parted, a tear formed in the corner of his eye and ran shakily down his cheek. Making an excuse about the car being double-parked, I left before he saw that my eyes were also beginning to mist over. Back in the car Heather asked how he was, and we travelled another 30 minutes before I could speak.

Chapter 4
Spain Here We Come

Upon arriving at Portsmouth docks we were informed that the ferry we had booked had been delayed for 3 hours, due to the force 9 gales it had encountered around the Bay of Biscay. Evidently that would be the same bay we would be travelling through on our way to Bilbao.

After walking through the ferry waiting area, Heather and I agreed to spend our time waiting inside the pub at the entrance to the ferry terminal. You couldn't have wished for a warmer welcome. The whole place was decorated for Christmas, Noddy Holder was blaring from the jukebox, and everybody was singing along. I turned to Heather, passing her the drink I had just ordered, and asked, "I wonder what we will be doing this time next year?" She shrugged her reply. Christmas has always been one of Heather's favourite times of the year, and probably for the first time since we started this roller coaster adventure over a year ago, I had the faintest hesitation and the flicker of "What the hell are we doing?"

The trip was to take 2 days, and within 5 hours of setting sail we were being bounced off the walls of the corridors as we tried to find our way around the ferry. Many of the passengers had booked the journey as a mini cruise, only staying in Bilbao for a few hours before re-boarding and setting off back to Blighty.

I think I had imagined that arriving in Bilbao would be a bit like stepping of the plane when visiting southern Spain in the summer, with glorious sunshine and the heat hitting you as you passed through the aircraft doors. I couldn't have been more wrong—it was absolutely pouring down and it was freezing cold.

We turned on my newly purchased GPS and asked it to navigate us directly to our destination. Our first port of call had been arranged before our departure. One of our neighbour's parents had a villa just outside Torrevieja and had arranged for us to rent the one next door for a month. Although we hadn't intended to live in that area, we had agreed to keep an open mind, and if all else failed we'd just use it as a holiday over Christmas and New Year.

We followed the directions of Miriam, the name we had christened the polite female guiding us from the GPS. Thirty minutes later we arrived back where we had started, in the docks at Bilbao. Heather said nothing but started to dig out a map. "I think I programmed it wrong," I confessed.

After a bit of tinkering Miriam was pointing us south toward the motorway. Within 20 miles we had seen 3 crashes, all vehicles that had lost control on sharp bends and slid into the barriers before overturning; the rain made driving treacherous.

After completing about half the distance from Bilbao to our destination we agreed to stop for a bite to eat. This was to be our first encounter with the locals. We walked into a ramshackle restaurant and sat down. The waitress approached and asked what we would like—well, I am presuming that is what she said. To say my Spanish was rusty would be a little of an understatement. Trying to keep it simple, I ordered chicken sandwiches for both of us. As I spoke and the waitress listened intently, I was getting the impression that during the time I had studied Spanish at night school, I had inadvertently been going into the Russian class each week.

The waitress looked at me with a blank expression and just smiled. I repeated my request. This time she smiled and walked away, and I smiled at Heather smugly. A minute later the waitress returned and handed me a menu. Heather returned my smug smile. Eventually we chose something off the list and we agreed to eat whatever came. I was close; it was their equivalent of our Sunday dinner and tasted wonderful.

As we left the restaurant the mobile phone rang. It was a call from Stacey and Ashlie. Before leaving the UK I had given them two pieces of advice. Firstly, if you are thinking of doing something and you don't think I would approve of it, then don't do it. Secondly, if you are determined to do something I wouldn't agree with, especially something dangerous, tell us after you have done it. "Don't text or e-mail us saying you are going bungee jumping the next day, then not contact us for a week," I had warned them.

The call started with the usual. "How are you and what have you been up to?" Then Stacey said, "We can tell you now because we have done it." I let her continue. "We rented a motorbike yesterday." I cringed; neither had ever been near a motorbike in their lives. "At first the locals found it hilarious because I kept mixing up the brake with the accelerator, but eventually I got the hang of it and we went up this narrow road heading for the jungle. Suddenly it started raining really heavy and the road just turned to mud, after falling off a couple of times we got back to the main road… It was great!"

"Speak to your mother," I said, passing the mobile to Heather. I had heard enough.

Back under the directions of Miriam, we turned onto the motorway and were once again heading south. Approaching a toll, Heather prepared the necessary change, paid, and off we went.

Five minutes later Miriam asked us to leave at the next exit. Heather reached for the map. "Have faith," I said, looking sideways while looking at the map. After following Miriam's advice of "Turn left, 2nd right," we were back on the motorway. "See, I told you to trust her."

Another 10 minutes passed and we approached another toll. "They were close together," Heather said. Then we realised it was the same one we had just been through; even the person collecting the money gave a knowing smile. "Is Miriam on bloody commission?" Heather asked. After that the map stayed on Heather's knee.

We arrived, at last, and had a very pleasant surprise. The villa was part of a new estate of very exclusive and very expensive homes, starting at about £300,000. It was a 3 bedroom detached villa with gardens and its own pool, although the water in the pool was far too cold. The weather had picked up as we had driven further south and now almost as far south as you can go it was a comfortable 17 degrees. The villa also had access to the internet so we checked to see if we'd received any e-mails.

E-MAIL
FROM Stacey/Ashlie
Hi.
Went to a bar last night called the 'Ping-Pong Bar'. Sounded interesting so Ash and I popped in for a drink. It was full of good looking young girls that we later found out were boys.... I couldn't believe it!

Then came on the act. A woman... A real woman was, whilst lying on the bar, firing ping-pong balls across the room using a certain part of her anatomy.

Going to Phuket and some other islands tomorrow for a few weeks.

Speak soon and let us know where you end up.
Stacey and Ashlie xxx

We met our neighbours that had arranged the accommodations, a sprightly pair, both retired but still full of life. Over the next few days they showed us around the local area and invited us to join some of their friends for a spot of lunch. We all met at a local restaurant that served a very nice *menu del dia*, a 3-course meal and drink for about the equivalent of £5 each. All their friends, we later found out, lived in the same complex and were all also retired.

Walking back to the cars en masse, one of them pointed out a local bar and stated, "We don't go in there."

"Why?" I asked.

"It's a bit Spanish," came his reply, and at that they all mumbled in agreement.

The next day we all gathered at one of the friend's house for drinks, quite a few in fact. I asked one of the men, a retired army officer, how long he had lived in Spain. "7 years," was his reply.

"You must speak Spanish quite well then," I said, nodding.

"Not a word, don't need to around here, all the locals speak English." Once again those within earshot mumbled in agreement.

Later that night I relayed the conversation to Heather and she had had a similar response from some of her questions from the women at the gathering. It confirmed our suspicion that we needed to go inland to find the kind of Spain that we were looking for. Nevertheless I suggested driving around some of the new developments within our price range the next day.

That is exactly what we did for a whole morning. We drove up and down a development the size of a major city. We didn't spend that long because we were so impressed with it—no, we just couldn't find our way out. Even Miriam was no help as all the roads were so new that they weren't on her database. We couldn't even find anybody to ask; the whole place was deserted. We were later told that on average they are only ever 25% occupied, the majority being holiday homes.

That afternoon I rang my mother to see how my father was. The phone was answered by Michael, my nephew who lives with my parents. "Is my mother there?" I asked.

"You've not heard then?" My heart sank.

"What?" I asked not really wanting to know the answer, sure it was bad news about my father.

"She's in the hospital. She fell and broke a bone in her hand, they are operating on it this morning but she will be home by tea time." He waited for my reply.

"I'll ring back tonight."

I did ring back later and spoke to her. Although the injury wasn't serious it was just one more thing on her plate that she didn't need and you could tell by her voice.

A week later I rang an estate agent based in Granada that I had been corresponding with whilst back in the UK. We arranged to meet up for the day just west of Granada and look at a few properties.

We set off for the three and a half hour drive full of hope, arriving at the agreed meeting point just before lunch. Mike, a tall, young man who looked like he had stepped off the front of Vogue was waiting when we arrived. I didn't realise it was possible to dislike somebody just because they are better looking than you. "Mmm, the girls would like him," Heather said, staring for just a little bit too long.

We spent the rest of that day looking around various houses, although only one met all of our criteria. We both agreed this was the area we wanted to settle. At 6pm it started to get dark so after arranging to meet again in the New Year, we said our goodbyes to Mike and set off back to our posh villa in Brits Ville.

Christmas arrived and the residents of our villa complex departed. They had all booked a '4-day-deal' to spend Christmas in Benidorm. We gave our neighbours a lift to the coach station, a journey they spent apologising for leaving us on our own. "We would have booked you on it if we had known," they said repeatedly.

We spent the rest of the day a little further up the coast on the beach. As the sun went down we retuned to the car. Not quite sure exactly where we were, I programmed Miriam to take us back to San Miguel, the small village that housed our complex. It had only taken about 15 minutes to drive to the beach so when the return journey had lasted 35 minutes Heather asked, "Where the hell are we?" I glanced down to the GPS to see that, according to Miriam, we still had 738 miles to go. I didn't realise Spain had more than one town called San Miguel.

The girls sent another e-mail confirming that they were safely on terra firma, having moved on to Australia. The e-mail read:

E-MAIL
FROM Stacey/Ashlie
Hi yer,
We can tell you now that we are safely in OZ. To be honest we are glad to be out of Thailand, I don't know how much longer we could have survived.

This morning we went to the Melbourne gaol where Ned Kelly was hung. (Whoever he is!)

Ashlie got a bit of a scare when I asked her to wait on a bench whilst I nipped into a shopping centre for some magazines. I didn't return for over an hour. Apparently I went out of a different door to the one I went in and got myself lost.

We are back at the hostel now and just had a shower. Ashlie has just pointed out that for the last two days I have been using the 'Men's'…. Ooops.

Move on to Sydney at the end of the week.
Missing you both.
Stacey and Ash xxx

A few days later whilst watching television we saw how a couple of Thai fishermen were to be executed for raping and killing a young backpacker. This happened on the beach of one of the islands where Stacey and Ashlie had been staying.

In Spain over the Christmas period almost everything shuts down until after the 6th of January, 'All Kings Day' they call it, and this is the day the children open their presents, not the 25th December like the UK. Between Christmas and New Year I made several calls to Mike and asked if he would sort out some accommodation for us, preferably a 2-bedroom house for a month. That would enable us to put everything from the car in the spare bedroom. "Don't worry I'll sort everything for you," he said.

New Year came and once again we were invited to a function organised by our local residents. I must admit that both Heather and I had an excellent time; our new friends may not be able to mix with the locals but they certainly know how to mix their drinks.

The next day I received a text from Ashlie.

HAD A GREAT NIGHT LAST NIGHT. WENT PARTYING GOT ADOPTED BY SOME OLDIES WHO LOOKED AFTER US. X

I sent one back.

SAME HERE. X.

Later that same day we rang them and spoke to Stacey. She told us about what had happened after going to bed. A rumour had circulated that a possible terrorist attack may be attempted during the New Year celebrations. The explosion that occurred at about 4am had scared them both to death. They had both jumped out of bed and turned on the light. The fridge door swung limply on its hinges and there wasn't much left of the plastic door to the freezer compartment. But this is what happens when you put a couple of cans of Cola in the freezer... Isn't it Stacey?

I kept chasing Mike up with regards to our temporary accommodations. He had gone on holiday and passed the job to somebody else, who hadn't done anything about it.

"Don't worry, we will have something by the time you get here, it's quite difficult being Christmas," said one of his colleagues.

"This is why I gave you 2 weeks to do it," I replied. "We are coming over in 2 days."

"All in hand," came the confident reply.

Chapter 5
Andalucia

We packed our things and had a last meal with the golden oldies. I rang the estate agents and explained that we were setting off. "Do you have somewhere for us to stay?" I asked

"Somebody will meet you at the service station at just before junction 187," we were told.

After sitting at the service station for 30 minutes I rang them again.

"Err, yes, err right, I'll send somebody up," came the reply.

After another 30 minutes an old Land Rover drew alongside us, the window went down and out popped a head. "Alan and Heather, I presume?" I felt like Livingstone.

He continued, "We have had a slight problem finding you somewhere, being Christmas and all. What I have done is booked you in to a bed and breakfast for a week; it's run by a couple from Halifax."

We followed the battered Land Rover through the countryside, eventually arriving at a small village. After negotiating the narrow streets we pulled up outside a large, white townhouse. We were greeted by the owners but before we turned back to thank the driver, the Land Rover had gone. "Come inside doll," said Maureen, one of the owners. "This is my husband, Joe." I explained that all our possessions were in the car and asked if they had somewhere I could store them. "Of course doll, this way." I followed Maureen through the house to an extension on the back that doubled the size of the building. "We don't use this part of the house yet, you can leave it all in here doll."

After unloading the car we were told that there were no other visitors staying at the moment so we could use the entire top floor. "I can't show you up cos I've not been well and I can't do stairs, doll." I said that wasn't a problem and Heather and I climbed the stairs to find our own room. At the top was a tiny room with a small portable television and video recorder, and the bedrooms and bathroom led off from there.

By now it was beginning to turn dark and although it might be 17 degrees on the coast, where we were now was much higher, almost in the mountains. That meant that when the sun went down so did the temperature, dramatically. We sat down to watch the television, which was not plugged into an aerial. "Never mind," I said, "there are some videos here." Now I'm not sure if it was because the television was faulty, the video player was ancient, the video was a bad quality, or if it was the fact that my ears had nearly frozen off, but you just couldn't make out what the people were saying. We tried a couple of different videos but the effect was just the same. The temperature began to drop even further. "God I'm cold," Heather said.

"So am I doll," I replied, and at that we both just cracked out laughing.

By 9pm the temperature had dropped below freezing and the house, as I could see, had no heating. I went downstairs to ask our hosts if there was a mobile heater, as were popular in many Spanish houses.

I knocked on the door of their private quarters and immediately the door opened. "Come in doll," Maureen said, brandy glass in one hand and cigarette in the other. As I stepped in I thought I had entered a taproom. The air was so thick with smoke. I pictured Jack the Ripper hiding in the corner awaiting his next victim. Before I spoke, Joe said, "I bet you're freezing up there, aren't you? We only have the one heater you see," he said, pointing to one at his feet. That answered my question. "You can use the quilts off the beds in the unused bedrooms if it will help."

"Thanks," I said and departed. I climbed the steps wondering how I was going to break this to Heather. If anything put her in a bad mood it was being cold. For the next hour we wrapped ourselves up in the 3 or 4 quilts we could salvage from the other bedrooms and tried to lip read *Jaws 2*. If we spoke you could see the condensation from our breath. Unable to stand it any longer, we went to bed vowing to either find somewhere else to stay or purchase a couple of hot water bottles.

The next day we met up with Mike, who had returned from his holiday. He apologised profusely for the fact that no accommodations had been organised before we had arrived. We explained about how unbearable the cold was at MoJo's B&B, as it was called. He explained that it was a very busy time of year but that he had a villa he could rent us next to his house. "It's a bit out of the way though. I'm not sure the road would be suitable for your car."

Knowing it would probably be another few months before we found somewhere, and moved in, we were willing to try anything. We followed him to a service station, locked up our car, and jumped in to his brand spanking new 4-wheel drive. After about 40 minutes I said to Heather. "Well it's a bit out of the way but the road doesn't seem too bad." He then swung the steering wheel around and crossed the field to our left. Bad, but I was still convinced that my car could make it. Then he left the field and started to climb the mountain, in the car!

Another 30 minutes of bouncing around—and it was anybody's bet what went first, the axles or my stomach—and turning a corner, we pulled up outside a small, isolated farmhouse complete with swimming pool. We stepped out of the car to total silence. We could have been on another planet, not a sound. Mike showed us around, looked at me and said, "Your car wouldn't make it, would it?"

"No," I was sorry to say. The place was fantastic. Still feeling a bit guilty about our plight at MoJo's, Mike went into the house and came back out carrying a large electric radiator. "Perhaps this will make things a bit more comfortable."

We returned to the B&B wondering how we were going to smuggle our newly found treasure up to our room. We couldn't just walk in with it or our hosts may take offence. We decided to sneak down after dark.

"How did the house hunting go doll?" was the greeting we received on returning to the B&B. Maureen stood at the entrance to the private quarters once again with glass and cigarette in hand. "Fine," I answered.

"I'm sorry it's so cold upstairs at night but these houses are built to keep out the heat in summer; we would buy another heater but the electric is so old we can only have 3 things running at a time, so there would be no point."

Foiled again.

We actually managed to stay at MoJo's for 6 days before Mike found us somewhere on the coast. When it came time to repack the car and say our goodbyes I realised that we still had the heater in the car. I dragged Heather to one side. "We still have that heater in the car that Mike lent us."

So," Heather said. "What's the problem? We will give him it back next time we see him."

"The problem is…" I continued speaking out of the side of my mouth whilst Maureen looked over suspiciously. "The car holds everything we brought from home and nothing else. It won't all fit in. I put the car rug over the heater, packed everything around it, and pretended to look astonished when the car was full and we still had several things lying on the pavement. "Don't know what's happened there," I said, worthy of an Oscar. "Oh just come back for it another day doll," said Maureen.

"Thanks." We climbed into the car, asked Miriam to take us to Benalmadena, and off we went.

I can imagine you wondering what essential items you would take with you in our position, especially when space is so limited. Well, as I said earlier, most things we had to sell, like the toaster, iron, kettle, video recorder, and many things that it would have been handy to have when setting up a new home. Somehow we ended up packing some things that perhaps, on reflection, should have been lower down on the priority list, like:

A dartboard.

An optics drink dispenser.

The shells we collected from the beach in Portugal last year.

A sewing basket. Heather hasn't sewed for 20 years.

A boogie board.

A bike carrier for a car (no bikes).

Hindsight's a wonderful thing!

Arriving at Benalmadena, Mike took us to what would be our home until we found our dream house. The Miramar apartments are a large nondescript block, but clean and tidy. The only problem was it was about 1 mile from the coast and what felt like 5,000 feet up the hillside.

A text received from Ashlie read:

ME AND STACEY GONNA BE IN NATIONAL NEWSPAPER, PICTURES AS WELL. WILL TELL U MORE IN E-MAIL.

It was 2 days before I could get to an Internet café. The e-mail included a photograph of the newspaper; she was right, it did include a picture of them both. The article was a debate on the accessibility of contraception and the morning after pill. Under each smiling, tanned face was the reply they gave when asked their opinion. Both answers reflected the fact that they were mature adults and that if it was available to anybody at any age, people would have sex 'willy-nilly'. I'm sure the pun wasn't intentional and I was hoping they were practising what they were preaching.

Our apartment was roomy, clean, and airy. (I'm starting to sound like an estate agent now.) The one drawback was the neighbour above us. She would come home at all hours of the night and insisted on wearing her high heels all the time. Heather, who I thought was fast asleep next to me, said without opening her eyes, "One thing's for sure, we are not buying an apartment."

For the next 2 weeks we visited dozens of houses, all different in shape, size, and location. We spent hours looking through estate agents' windows. What amazed me about the pictures advertising the houses for sale was how amateurish they were. When the photographer had visited our house back in the UK he had spent some time moving furniture around to make the rooms look bigger. We cleaned and polished and made sure the garden was spotless. This is most definitely not the case in Spain. Heather pointed out a photograph in one window showing a house that was for sale for quite a lot of money. The picture was of the living room and in the middle was a man lying on the couch reading a newspaper with his other hand down his trousers.

On one occasion when looking around a property the owner stopped at a door and said in broken English, "My mother, she is asleeping in this bedroom but it is not a *problema* if we are most quiet."

A typical picture advertising a property's kitchen would show the sink piled high with dirty pots. When you think that some of the estate agents work on fees of up to 20% you would expect a little more for your money. It is also possible to have the same house for sale with as many as 50 different estate agents all offering the property at various prices, unlike in the UK where many sellers demand exclusive rights of sale.

Much of the time spent at Benalmadina between house hunting was spent playing tourists down on the promenade. At this time of the year it was relatively quiet, except for the retired folk who were spending winter in warmer climates. These people could be found going up and down the prom in matching electric buggies or walking quickly with the aid of ski poles. I was dying to shout to tell them they had lost their skis.

A local paper had a letter from an elderly Brit who lived full time on the coast. He was complaining that his winter fuel allowance had been taxed. The answer, instead of reprimanding him for using up funds allocated for the genuine needy back in the UK, gave him a half page explanation as to how he could use a loophole in the system and receive it in full.

Text from Stacey;

CAN'T TELL YOU WHAT ASH IS DOING ON MONDAY. DON'T THINK YOU WOULD APPROVE BUT WILL E-MAIL PICTURES ON TUESDAY.

It was only Saturday. It was going to be a long weekend.

We left it until quite late on the Tuesday, taking into consideration the time difference, but once at the Internet café I typed away eagerly wanting to know what they were up to now.

The picture was of Ashlie in scuba diving gear with a 12 ft shark, teeth shining right above her. The accompanying letter explained how, after a visit to an aquarium, Ashlie had seen a poster offering the opportunity to swim with sharks. The e-mail then went on to explain how at one stage she began to panic and the diving instructor had had to come across to her and hold her still. I'm now beginning to think that we probably won't need a 3-bedroom house next year.

After a great deal of consideration and discussion, Heather and I decided to put an offer in on a house that we had seen when we first came over for a day in December.

The offer was accepted and wheels were put in motion. The Spanish solicitor we were using had been recommended to us by the estate agents. (Mistake number 1).

They say that the attitude in Spain is *mañana, mañana* tomorrow, tomorrow. In truth this was one of the aspects of Spain's way of life that attracted me to the country. I wanted to escape the stress and the hustle and bustle of the UK. This is fine until you want something done. Our solicitor was taking forever and a day; in addition to this it was almost impossible to contact him. When we did it was never good news.

Whilst this was happening, we were looking at cars with the idea of selling my British model and buying a Spanish plated car. When I mentioned this to Mike, he asked, "Is there anything wrong with yours?"

"No," I replied. "But I thought you had to change it if you were staying more than 6 months."

"How do they know how long you have stayed in the country? You can go to Gibralter or France without anybody recording it, so if anybody asks just tell them that's what you do, leave the country every couple of months and you don't need to change it."

"What about road tax, etc?" I asked.

Mike smiled. "Why would you need road tax? You're not using it on a British road. I used my British car for nine years before changing it; as long as it's insured you're covered. Just have a look around and see how many British registered cars are driving around with no tax disc."

Now this seemed quite an inviting proposition especially when I was fully aware that I was going to lose a fortune when I sold my car over here in Spain. In fact, as I recalled, Maureen at MoJo's B&B had done and said the same. As I drove and walked around I was amazed at just how many British registered cars without tax discs there were.

The following morning I went out to my car to find that it had a flat tyre. Fifty yards away there was a petrol station. Now I know I shouldn't have, but I drove it the short distance and refilled it with air, just to see if it was a slow puncture that would allow me to drive it the mile or so to the tyre garage, rather than changing it myself. Fortunately it worked but still needed to be taken in and fixed.

The man at the garage looked at the tyre and said it would need to be replaced as the puncture was in the sidewall and unfixable. I followed him back into his office and waited for him to calculate the cost. "400 Euros," he said, turning his calculator around to prove it.

"What?" I questioned. "That's over twice as much as in the UK."

"That is because you require 2 new tyres," he replied with a cocky smile.

"But I only need one," I said, turning around and noticing that the tyre was by now looking decidedly flat.

"I cannot fit only one new one because on the other side the tyre opposite is almost bare and the grip on the road would be uneven, dangerous in fact."

I made a mental note to get the tattoo removed from my forehead that read: 'English mug'. I checked the other tyre and it was looking a little sparse in the way of tread, so I gave in and let him replace them both. This had also made my mind up for me; I would keep the car, especially now that I had just spent 400 Euros on it. (Mistake number 2).

We were beginning to get a bit despondent with how long the process was taking on the house. We were told it would probably take about 3 weeks, and we were now into the 5th and renting the apartment was eating into our savings. "Let's cheer ourselves up, let's go down to the call box and ring some of our friends in the UK."

Thirty minutes later we had been updated with news from home. My father had had a difficult week and his speech hadn't improved. A friend of mine was in the hospital having an operation on his kidneys. His wife had been told she also had to have an operation on her feet. A friend of Heather's had lost the baby she was carrying, and the doctor Heather had worked for had been diagnosed with terminal cancer. If nothing else the phone call put our problems into perspective.

Checking our e-mail the following day, we had received two. The first was from Stacey and Ashlie. It explained how, through an agency, they had both managed to secure work at the same place. However, the place was a small town called Kracow, about 250 miles into the outback. The village was basically a gold mine. I don't mean it was a good place to earn money; the place was an actual gold mine. The only things there were the accommodations for the workers and a bar/cafe. As I read on I had my fingers crossed that the job they had been offered was in the bar and not the mine. The job was in fact to get up at 5am to make the breakfasts for the miners and in the evening to serve behind the bar. Stacey's only concern was the fact that the nearest shops were over 35 miles away. I can't deny I had one or two other reservations. The e-mail mentioned that because of the remoteness of the place they would be out of contact for the whole of the next month, as that was how long they had the jobs for.

Heather spoke without taking her eyes of the screen. "So let me make sure I've read this right. My two babies are heading 250 miles into the Australian outback to work behind a bar, in a town that has nothing else but dirty miners in it, and, we won't be hearing from them for a month!"

"Sounds like it," I said in an unconvincing, happy voice. "So much for showing them the *Wolf Creek* movie," I added.

We both read the second e-mail in silence. It was from Heather's sister Anne, explaining that Pamela, who was looking after our two cats, was having a horrendous time, to the extent that she had needed to take some time off work to cope.

Several years earlier Pamela had looked after one of our cats whilst we were on holiday. One day it went out and didn't return. As a consequence she dared not let these two out, and they were making a complete mess of her house, including taking chunks out of her own cat when she wasn't about. Something had to be done. So we arranged for them to be sent over to us and placed in a cattery. We couldn't take them straight away because we had decided to make a trip back to England at the end of the month.

After reading the e-mails we decided we needed a drink, so we made our way to a pleasant looking bar in a nearby square. After being served we sat in silence, pondering over the e-mail from the kids. As if from nowhere, behind our heads a busker strummed his guitar and began singing.

"Don't worry... about a thing.... Cos every little thing, is gonna be alright."

I think that must have been the biggest tip I've ever given a busker.

Being totally frustrated about the delay in the house, combined with the fact that over the last week or so our solicitor had stopped returning our calls, I made a call to Mike at the estate agents'. I explained that if the house hadn't gone through by the following Friday, the deal was off. Amazingly we were informed later that day that everything was ready and an appointment had been made for the Monday for us to attend at the Notary.

The Notary is the place where all the transactions are registered, all the deeds are signed and exchanged, and the money handed over. Research had told us that when purchasing a house in Spain the actual figure agreed is not the amount handed over. For example if you purchase a house for €100,000, then maybe €70,000 is the figure that appears on the paperwork and €30,000 is handed over in cash. This means that the tax paid by both the seller and the buyer is reduced. Having spoken to many people over the previous months, everybody had carried out their transactions in this way. Of course we didn't get involved in such shady dealings.

We arrived at the Notary and sure enough there were another 6 parties all waiting for their turn to be seen. Amongst each party there was an individual carrying a supermarket bag filled with cash. My immediate thought was if everything goes wrong with our new life in Spain, then I am buying a gun and coming back to hold this place up. I can just see the police asking what the robber had stolen and all the victims looking at each other, afraid to admit that they had lost thousands because they were in the process of carrying out a tax fiddle.

I was amazed when I looked around the office to see all the secretaries using manual typewriters—not a computer in sight. Maybe if things don't work out I won't have to turn to a life of crime, I could send Heather to work there.

Once the contracts had been signed and cheques had been swapped for keys, I explained to our solicitor that we are setting straight off to the house to deposit all our worldly belongings in our new garage. From there we are going to drive back to the UK for 2 weeks. He had already agreed to sort out the connection of water and electricity and set up our direct debits to pay these bills. (Mistake number 3).

Chapter 6
Back to Blighty

Because we had decided to keep the car, we chose to drive back to the UK and return with some of the things we had intended to leave in long-term storage in Pamela's cellar. There were no ferries available from Bilbao so we had to drive all the way up through Spain and France.

We had arranged to stay at one of Heather's friend's houses and all things considered we were quite looking forward to seeing everybody. On this occasion we were unable to rely on the trusty GPS and Miriam, because 3 weeks earlier I had allowed the battery to run down and somehow lost the entire database. A problem my brother would resolve before our return.

We drove long, fast, and hard and managed to get back to Leeds 3 days later; not bad considering all of Spain was recovering from 8 inches of snow dropped the previous day.

After pre-warning everybody of our homecoming, I had also asked that nobody tell my mother; I wanted to surprise her. About 10 minutes away from her house I rang to see if she was going to be in during the next 15 minutes. When she asked why? I explained that I didn't have much credit left on my phone card and I didn't want it to run out in mid-conversation, as had happened a day or so earlier. "Yes," she said. "I'm not going anywhere." My sister had e-mailed me several weeks earlier to tell me that my mother was now under the doctor for stress brought on by looking after my father. I could tell by her voice she was feeling down.

Heather and I parked the car half way down her street and rang her from my mobile. When she answered I went through the usual conversation of asking how everybody was, all the time sneaking up the street and into the house. I could see her on the phone in the hall. "And how are you?" I asked.

Oh, missing you," she answered. At that I tapped her on the shoulder. She spun around.

"Oh my God, you stupid bugger!" She yelled with a combination of surprise, shock, and excitement. "I nearly had a bloody heart attack!" My life of crime was developing fast; one minute I'm thinking of robbery, the next I nearly murder my own mother. Once she had calmed down she called my father down from upstairs. He walked steadily into the room and asked if we wanted a cup of tea. "That's one thing I've missed," I said with complete honesty. His speech had improved slightly although he did struggle a couple of times. His breathing was also quite laboured, but his tea was just how I'd remembered it, lovely.

Whilst in the UK we didn't want to spend our time visiting people so we sent it through the necessary grapevines that everybody was invited to the local pub at 7pm the following Friday. We spruced ourselves up and went down to the pub at 8pm expecting to make a big entrance. Inside there was nobody except a couple of drunks that looked like they had been there since dinnertime. Looking a bit embarrassed, the friends we were staying with, who had accompanied us down, asked, "Are you sure you told people it was this pub?"

We got a drink in and friends started to show up. An hour later the place was packed with friends and relatives.

With the car packed once again to the roof, including a set of solar garden lights and 2 sun lounges bought on special offer from B&Q, we were ready to set back off. Our visit had flown by. It didn't feel like a week ago we had said goodbye to our friends in the pub, with an offer of a free holiday and the phrase used by the famous holiday camp owner, Fred Pontin, "Book early to avoid disappointment."

After an overnight visit to my brother's in Bury St. Edmunds, to break-up the journey and get Miriam up and running, we were once again on our way. We had decided to make the return trip a little more leisurely and spread it over 4 or 5 days.

France was pleasant, though I couldn't help but wonder why the French were so much against the British, especially as I drove past the dozens of cemeteries containing the 1000s of dead young British soldiers that had died trying to deliver freedom to France.

Bored of Miriam's polite but mundane muttering, I decided to have a little tinker with the GPS. My brother had mentioned that he had added a couple of new voices, so I went through the options trying to find them. Eventually I located them and chose a new one at random, replaced the GPS on the dashboard, and waited to see who was going to give us our new directions. Within seconds a slightly slurred, maybe even drunk, male voice with a Brummy accent announced, "Err at the next fucking roundabout take the 2nd fucking exit." Heather and I just looked at each other. I had programmed it to avoid motorway charges and as we approached a fork in the road that gave you an option of the motorway or not, the new voice directed us away with, "Keep to the lllleft.... Fffucking chargessss." We christened our new, inebriated navigator as Spider. Only later did we find out that it was supposed to be Ozzy Osbourne.

Climbing the mountains to the north of Madrid I had a distinct feeling that there was a slight drop in power. The road climbed and climbed until we disappeared into low cloud. The car began to slow down; I pushed the accelerator to the floor but to no avail. We were still slowing down. By now Heather realised that there was definitely something wrong. "What's happening?" she asked.

"The car's dead. The engine's conked out," I replied. Although on entering the cloud I had switched on my head and fog lights, my biggest fear was a car running into the back of us at a high speed. As we free-wheeled to the crest of the hill I could feel myself subconsciously rocking my head and shoulders back and forward in an effort to help it over. We slowed to a near stop, just as we reached the crest. Slowly the car began to pick up speed and we began to roll down the other side. Coming out of the cloud I looked into my rear view mirror to see we were producing our own cloud.

Thick smoke poured from the exhaust. Further down the hill was a conveniently placed slip road. I pulled off and stopped.

Before returning to the UK my car insurance had run out, so through a Spanish company I had renewed it and fortunately paid an additional 35 Euros to add breakdown recovery.

My mobile had only a little credit left so I had to make the call quick and effective. Before calling I used the GPS to locate our exact position and name of the road. Whilst doing this, Spider announced, "You've gone the wrong fucking way, turn around." Just for a second my temper got the better of me and I lost my composure.

"Fuck off yourself!" I cried.

"Do you speak English?" I asked on the mobile.

"*Un momento*," came the reply. Eventually, in broken English, I was asked what it was I wanted. Having rung the breakdown service I thought the answer was quite obvious and was just about to say so when I remembered I had limited time to speak. I explained slowly what the problem was and using the GPS gave the exact junction and asked if the operator would be so good as to call me back. "I is sorry I is not understanding you." I sighed and repeated my problem and location and asked once again if I could be called back. "I is still not understanding you sir." I was very tempted to put Spider on the line. I repeated everything for the third time. "Ah I am seeing. I is ringing you back sir."

After five minutes the operator rang back. Another ten minutes later we agreed on my position. "We am sending man to be seeing you in next hour, sir."

Almost to the minute, an hour later I looked in my rear view mirror and said to Heather, "Here they come." A large blue pickup truck pulled in behind us. At that very same moment a large green pickup turned the corner in front of us, indicated, and pulled up to my bonnet. "This is going to be interesting." I said.

Both drivers got out of their cabs and walked slowly toward each other. It looked like a scene from *High Noon*. The discussion started warmly and quietly but soon escalated into a shouting match. Heather suggested I get out and find out what's going on. Sheepishly I flicked the bonnet switch and got out and said hello.

Both mechanics stopped talking, looked at me, muttered something to each other, and smiled. "What is being the *problema?*" one asked. I explained about the loss of power and the smoke gushing out of the exhaust. They looked at the engine and once again began muttering to each other in a whisper. "When is it you last put in the petrol?" By now it was obvious that only one of them spoke any English and he was using this advantage to claim the job. The other, accepting defeat shook his head, returned to his truck, and drove off. "I filled up about twenty miles back," I answered.

"I is thinking that this is the *problema*, you are not putting the correct petrol in the car." I knew his diagnosis was wrong because I had filled the car myself and made sure I had used '*Sin Plumo*', lead free.

"I is taking you and your car to garage. Please be getting in my vehicle."

Thirty minutes later, Heather and I were grabbing a coffee while the mechanic at the garage looked over our car. "Right, let's go and get the verdict," I suggested to Heather.

The verdict was that this garage couldn't find what was wrong and the car would need to go to a Saab dealer. Unfortunately it was now three o'clock on a Saturday and nothing would be open until Monday. A quick call to the breakdown company, whose small print included completion of journey in the event of breakdown, and I was informed that a taxi would be sent to pick us up and take us to the Madrid airport, about fifty miles away, where we would be given a hire car.

As we headed south from the airport in the small 'Cleo', we left behind not only our car but also almost its entire contents. We had no idea when we would see it again. We had also been told that the hire car was only ours for twenty four hours and after that it would have to be returned to Granada airport, about thirty miles away from our new house.

Chapter 7
Welcome to Casa Cuthies

By the time we arrived at our new home it was dark, we were both completely shattered, and I had a migraine. "Don't worry. When we get in I'll make you a nice cup of tea," Heather said.

"Don't forget," I added. "We don't have a bed yet, we need to blow up that inflatable mattress." Although at the moment we had no furniture at all, we had in fact ordered a couple of beds whilst we were down on the coast, but unfortunately they weren't due until tomorrow. Speaking of which, we had invested €800 on a bed with a so called 'memory mattress'. It wasn't until several months later that I found out I had bought the only one in Spain to get Alzheimer's... it was rubbish.

We parked the car in the garage and went into the house. I turned the light on. Well that's not completely accurate, I flicked the light switch but nothing happened. I felt my way across the hall and did the same to another just in case there was a fault or no bulb in the first. Nothing. "Welcome to *Casa Cuthies*," I said with a sigh.

The fact that we had no electricity made me wonder if the water had been turned on. I fumbled my way to the downstairs toilet and turned the tap. Nothing.

I returned to the garage and managed to find a torch and between us we sat in the empty front room and took turns at blowing up the airbed. It was freezing cold.

When the job was done, still in our clothes, we snuggled down under the continental quilt we had bought earlier. "I'm sure it will all sort itself out tomorrow. I'll get on to the solicitor and find out what's happening."

At 5am I woke to find myself even colder. The airbed had gone down and we were lying on the cold floor tiles. Half asleep, I turned over. "Jesus Christ!" I jumped a mile. Heather must have also felt the cold during the night because she had pulled the hood of her fleece over her head and pulled the drawstrings tight, leaving only her nose and mouth showing. I wondered what the hell it was.

The first thing we had to do the next day was take the hire car to Granada airport. The breakdown company had agreed to pay for a taxi to bring us all the way back. The 35 Euros I had spent taking out the breakdown cover was probably the best investment I have ever made.

Hire car returned and back at the house we had to work out how we were going to survive without water and electricity—oh yes, and no car either. The water situation was solved by me making ten trips a day to the village tap. Armed with two red buckets, purchased from the small, local shop, off I would go and then stand for ten minutes while the slow tap did its job. Each trip seemed to attract more and more curious glances from the locals. I'm sure that people came out of the bar next to the tap just to watch. "Hola," I would say. This inevitably brought a mumbled reply that I'm sure translated to, "English nutter" or something similar.

Being the forever pessimist, I had bought a camping stove on our recent trip to the UK. I was glad I'd had the foresight to remove it from our car and bring it home with us in the hire car. So soup was the order of the day.

On Monday morning I rang the solicitor and asked where our water and electricity was. "On its way," he replied, "but it takes time."

I rang the garage about our car and was told that it was being transferred to a Saab dealer in Granada and within the next few days I should receive a call from them.

Our village is about five miles from the nearest town so I suggested to Heather that we take a leisurely stroll, pick up some supplies, and then get a taxi back. She agreed and off we went. We decided to take a back road out of the village and also use this expedition to explore our surroundings. As we walked down the road we noticed a large building with a pagoda and several chairs outside. "Looks like a bar we didn't know about," I said to Heather.

Up to then we thought the village only had the two bars on the main road. As we got closer, Heather said, "Looks more like some sort of clinic." She said this because outside in one of the chairs was a middle-aged woman with her leg in a pot and resting on a chair in front of her. On her lap was a kitten wearing one of those coned collars that vets put on to prevent them from licking a wound. As we got level with her, a man came out of the building, hair uncombed, unshaven, and wearing old clothes. Upon closer inspection they looked English. Never one to be slow at coming forward, I asked, "English?"

"No. Scottish," came the reply from the man. I was a little taken back, and then he smiled.

"I thought we were the only Brits in the village," I said in the Welsh accent used on the comedy *Little Britain*.

After a brief conversation we explained that we were walking to the town because we had no car at the moment. The dishevelled Scottish chap said he would be going in to town for his Spanish lesson and would give us a lift, but that would be in about an hour's time. "No it's okay," I said. "The walk will do us good." Out of the corner of my eye I could see Heather's expression, it was one of bewilderment. "Well if you need a lift back I will be outside the supermarket at about 1pm." With a thanks and a wave, off we went.

One and a half hours and about 4 miles later, the temperature was up into the mid twenties. We were sweating like mad and probably only two thirds of the way there. A car pulled up alongside and stopped. I had to do a double take before I realised that it was the scruffy Scot we were speaking to earlier. He now sat in the car, white shirt, clean shaven and combed hair. He was like a totally different person. "Need that lift?" he asked, knowing damn well we wished we had accepted it in the first place.

The rest of the journey was to take only another ten minutes but during that time proper introductions and backgrounds were exchanged. It turned out that Hugh, as he was called, had just retired from the British army as a Major, not that you would have guessed a couple of hours earlier. One thing was for sure: we would be taking him up on the offer of a lift back to our village.

A phone call later that day was from a garage in Granada to explain that they had my car, had looked at it and had deduced that it requires a new turbo. "How much will that cost?" I asked.

The reply came back in that broken English I was now beginning to believe was taught in schools instead of the Queen's English.

"Wan hundred," said the mechanic. I couldn't believe my luck, one hundred Euros was about seventy pounds; I had expected at least three times that.

"No, no I am very sorry," he added. "I am meaning wan *mil.*" A *mil* in Spanish is a thousand in English. The bill had just gone up ten times. To be honest he could have said "Two *mil.*" and I would have had to agree; the guy had me over a barrel. So agree I did and by the end of the week I had the car back. An added bonus was the solar garden lights I'd bought back in England. I found these in the back with everything else. This meant I could put them out during the day and at night time we had the house illuminated for the first time.

Four days later whilst recovering from another trip to the village tap there was a knock at the door. I opened it and found a man in overalls who began gibbering in very fast Spanish. I did catch one word, '*agua*'. I then noticed a motif on his breast pocket that I recognised to be the emblem of the local water authority. I interrupted him. "*Agua?*" I asked.

"*Sí,*" he replied. To his complete dismay I jumped as high as I could, punched the air, and shouted, "Yessss!" He took a step back and looked like he was going to do a runner. I gathered my composure and escorted him to where the meter was to be installed. Thirty minutes later we actually had running water. I was on a roll now. I thought I'd give the solicitor a ring to chase up the electricity.

"Have you not checked your e-mails Mr. Cuthbertson?" This sounded ominous.

"No not for the last couple of days, why?"

"Ah, I sent you one explaining that we have a problem with having your electricity connected." I didn't like the way this conversation was going. "A week after you bought the property a new law came in with very strict specification on the wiring of new houses, and apparently yours needs one or two changes." This I found totally unbelievable, as anybody who has visited Spain, especially inland, would find electricity wires hanging everywhere, partly due to the fact they don't put any underground as in the UK. I have seen houses where cables are running through a house held together with sellotape. "But it's a brand new house, how can this be so?"

"Ah but Mr. Cuthbertson it is not yet connected to the main supply and the rule applies to every house that is connected after a certain date."

"How much?" I realised this was a phrase I was going to have to learn in Spanish; it seemed to be one I was going to use quite a lot.

"I have obtained a quote for you Mr. Cuthbertson. Fortunately most of the work is to be done outside."

"How much?" I could sense this was going to be bad.

"Two thousand four hundred Euros."

Being placed continually over this barrel was beginning to play havoc with my back.

"Best tell them to get on with it," I said dejectedly.

Since we had arrived in the village we had only frequented one of the two bars. On each visit the place seemed to be full of only men, leaning on the bar or playing dominos, smashing them down each time and staring aggressively at their opponents.

Heather, being slightly old fashioned, said she didn't feel very comfortable being the only female. I suggested that maybe it was tradition and the women didn't go out and were supposed to stay at home while the husbands did all the socializing. Fortunately none of the patrons that night spoke English or Heather's reply of "They can go and bollocks" might have turned one or two heads, or even given them the excuse to ban her and return the bar to equilibrium. I then suggested to Heather that maybe the men were a little nervous that when their wives saw you in the bar, they may demand to come out, and thus begins the 'revenge of the *Las Stepford* wives.' I won't repeat her reply.

Speaking of Spanish traditions in the bar, a popular one in Spain is *Tapas*. This is a small snack that comes free with each drink that you buy, especially in Andalucia. Some of the concoctions were unidentifiable, but trying not to offend we would at least try each one. On more than one occasion Heather would retrieve a couple of half eaten bits from her handbag the following day. She was scared stiff of offending the staff by just leaving it. Sometimes this would back fire and when the barman saw her empty plate he would mistakenly think she had wolfed it down and bring her another, larger portion.

We had arranged to meet the Scottish couple, Sylvia and Hugh, in the other bar the following night and were pleasantly surprised— or, should I say, Heather was because the clientele were both male and female.

We had arrived early and sat down at a table near the door facing each other. A small group of people were crowded around a couple of tables behind ours. A few minutes later a man from this group stood up and came over to us. He gestured that he wanted us to lift our glasses from the table; I presumed he was going to wipe it or something. Imagine my surprise when he picked the table up and placed it next to the ones his friends were using. Heather and I sat facing each other holding our drinks not quite knowing what to do. Had we sat in somebody else's place? Were foreigners not welcome? After positioning our table, the Spanish man returned and asked me to stand up. I would be lying if I didn't admit that the phrase "I'm gonna get my head kicked in" wasn't running through my mind. He then dragged our chairs over to the table he'd put next to his friends and asked us to join them. We introduced ourselves and were made to feel very welcome. It gave me an excellent opportunity to practice my rusty Spanish; I also found out just how rusty it was. This was our first meeting with Antonio, later to be christened by us as Lee Van Cleef. Why? He was the spitting image of the 'Spaghetti Western' actor. When I pointed this out he took it as a great compliment.

Sylvia and Hugh arrived with their twelve-year-old daughter Emma. Because they had been in Spain a year, Sylvia and Hugh had picked up a bit of Spanish and in addition they were attending lessons in Loja, the local town. Emma was a natural, and within the year she had mastered the language to perfection, including all the hand gestures, which I later learned are just as important as the speech.

"Bingo starts at 10pm," said Sylvia.

"I don't know about that, I'm not sure I can remember all my numbers," I said, presuming correctly that the calling was going to be in Spanish.

"Don't worry, one of the locals will watch over your shoulder and if you miss one will give you a nudge."

This became a regular weekly night out, and not only did it give us an opportunity to meet and mix with the locals but it was also excellent practice for speaking Spanish, especially learning numbers.

The bar was tended by a father and son, both named Fernando, the elder of which I couldn't understand a word he said. His Spanish had such an Andalucian accent, it again sounded more like Welsh. His wife spent the evenings in the kitchen making the *tapas*. Can you imagine that in an English pub? "I've got an idea love, instead of watching *Eastenders*, you can spend the night cooking in the kitchen and we will give the food away to the punters." Yer right.

I found that each time I went to the bar I had to explain that I wanted a Bacardi with diet Coke and no ice. To save time I explained to the bar staff that in England this drink is called 'a usual'. From then on, I would just go to the bar and ask for "*usual, por favor.*" It made life a lot simpler for everybody. That is, until somebody else comes in and asks for their usual and ends up with the wrong drink.

To show how friendly the locals are, I happened to mention in conversation that we were living with no electricity, to emphasise the point I pulled a small torch, fastened to my key ring, out of my pocket and said, "This is the only light we have." The next thing I knew I was being frog marched out of the bar and across to a house where the owner spent ten minutes looking for a large torch for me to borrow.

Word must have travelled fast because everywhere we went we were asked if we had power yet. The brother of the person we bought the house from must have been receiving an ear bashing, even though it wasn't his fault, because one night in the bar he approached me rather sheepishly and offered to run a cable from his house to ours, two hundred metres away.

The workmen arrived the following week to sort out the electricity. It was explained that they needed to dig a trench about twenty feet long and lay some new cable. Watching them was like having a tooth pulled. The digging took four days, and when they had finished the top was delicately cemented over. After they had gone I went out to examine the workmanship. As I said they had cemented the trench and smoothed it over with amazing precision, then in letters six inches high had autographed it: ADRIAN & MANUEL. It looked... different, but we still didn't have any electricity; the electricity company had to fit the meter.

The light offered by the solar garden lights was, to be honest, pretty pathetic, and as our budget and livers prevented us from going to the bar every night, it was agreed that we might as well go to bed when it got dark. That was 8 o'clock. So when the clocks were put forward an hour for spring it meant that we could stay up until 9 o'clock.

One thing I've realised in Spain is that I am now very easily pleased.

E-MAIL
FROM Stacey/Ashlie
Back in civilisation now, we absolutely loved working out at the mine. Most of the blokes were about your age dad, although there were a few younger ones. We had to get up at God knows what time to make their breakfasts before they went to work. We now know how to fry an egg!

We had great fun in the bar on a night it wasn't really like working, but we had a lot of late nights. In the end we took it in turns to get up and do the breakfasts. This didn't always work as some times none of us got up and the miners ended up going to work having only had cereal, but they didn't mind.

Stacey and Ash xxx

A couple of weeks later we received a copy of the Australian mining magazine in the mail. Yes, you've guessed: On page five were Stacey and Ashlie, complete with overalls and helmets, down a mine getting ready to blow it. Along with the magazine was a note that explained how, having got tickets to see an episode of *Neighbours* being filmed, they had arrived late and ended up watching it from the green room with the cast not yet required for filming. They had all then gone on to a party taking them with them.

I had recently read a book about a couple who had bought a property in Spain without any power or water—déjà vu. This had recently become my bible. The amount of ideas I borrowed from the book were incredible, like putting water in plastic bottles in the sun to warm up and, hey presto, a warm shower. I forgot who the author was but he certainly made life for us that little bit easier.

Chapter 8
In the *Campo*

Whilst in the bar one night, Antonio (actually, from here on I'll call him Lee Van Cleef, because nearly every male in the village is called Antonio) patted me on the back and said in Spanish that he would pick me up tomorrow at my house at 12 o'clock.

"*¿Porqué?*" Why? I asked.

"*¡Hombre festival!*" he replied.

"*¿Hombre festival?*" I repeated. At this a group of men at the bar swivelled in their seats, raised their glasses, and cheered. "*¡Hombre festival!*" I agreed and asked if it would be okay for my Scottish friend, Hugh, to come along.

"*Sí,*" said Lee Van Cleef, "*Pero no—*" He then pointed to the females around the table and shook his forefinger from side to side.

"Looks like a man only do," I said to Heather, trying to hide a grin that was forcing its way out of the side of my mouth. "How long does it last?" I asked, turning back to Van Cleef.

"*Dos días,*" 2 days, came the reply.

Heather turned to one of the women at the table and asked, "What do the women do?" They all looked at each other in puzzlement, not because they didn't understand the question, it was just that nobody had ever asked it before. Heather's eyes scanned the ladies present, her forefinger pointing at the table in front of her, and she announced, "*Mañana aquí, a las ocho.*" Here tomorrow 8pm. The gathered females smiled in agreement. It's amazing how bilingual Heather can become when the need arises.

Hugh and I waited with a combination of excitement and anticipation. I had neglected to tell him that the night before it had been requested that he wear a skirt. I think they meant his kilt but who the hell knows what a *Hombre festival* is?

A rickety old car pulled up outside my house and beeped its horn; we went outside and got in. The driver, a man, about seventy years old, I had never seen before. But his front seat passenger, a young man of about twenty, had been in the bar the previous night.

We climbed into the back, the car was started and the young passenger turned up the stereo as loud as it would go. As the speakers were on the back sill, Hugh and I were immediately deafened, but the old man just carried on driving as though nothing had happened. We had no idea where we were going. The car cut across the country and down some isolated lanes. "Have you ever read '*The Story of Burning Man*'? I asked Hugh, almost screaming to be heard.

"No, why?" he yelled back.

"Never mind." The book in question was one I had read some time ago but for some reason it had sprung to mind. It was about a man who had moved to a small village and was invited to the annual village party where a dummy was burnt on a bonfire, I can't remember why. During the burning the man had noticed the dummy's eyes move just as the flames engulfed it. Apparently a visitor was sacrificed each year.

The car turned down a track and into an olive grove. Out of nowhere appeared a large, white house. As the car stopped in the shade of one of the olive trees I asked, "Who lives here?" The old man driving turned off the engine, which also killed the stereo, turned and said, "It is Fernando's house but it is used only for fiestas."

There were already about a dozen men milling about preparing drinks and food, and over the next hour more appeared until the total was near thirty. Sitting in a large circle in the shade of the house, we all drank beer whilst Hugh and I explained the differences between Spain and the UK, everything from house prices to opening hours. Their questions were endless.

The barbecue was lit and various meats were passed around. Once again I had no idea what I was eating. I was sitting between the Fernandos; the elder would ask me a question, his son would translate it to a Spanish I could understand, I would think of the answer in English and translate it to Spanish for young Fernando, who would in turn tell his father what I had said. Although it sounds like a painful process it was in fact quite fun.

I noticed that everybody else had changed from drinking beer to red wine. I pointed this out to Hugh, who said, "I'm staying on the beer." I was just about to agree when Lee Van Cleef approached us, took our glasses, poured out the contents and replaced it with red wine. I looked at Hugh, "I guess we are on the wine now."

I happened to mention that we had renamed Antonio Lee Van Cleef due to their likeness and Hugh said, "That's funny, I was thinking that bloke over there looks like Russell Grant, the fortune teller." I laughed because I could see the resemblance straight away. Glancing across the table I nudged Hugh and said. "Who does he remind you of? I'll give you a clue: Paattttt."

"Frank Butcher, from *Eastenders*."

"Correct." This turned into a game we still play today.

Once the barbecue had finished somebody shouted, "The *paella* is ready!" We all got up and walked indoors. In the corner of one room was a pan that measured about four feet across on an open fire. Inside was a mixture of rice, chicken, and seafood. The locals were fighting over it. I had filled up on the barbecue, so politely turned it down. I looked around and wondered where they all put it; not one of them had an ounce of fat on him.

Once the *paella* was gone, the younger men split up into two smaller groups and a couple of card schools were underway. I looked on with curiosity, as the playing cards used were different than what we were familiar with. Old Fernando saw me watching and shook his head slowly from side to side. I then realised why; each player was throwing a fifty euro note on the table and he didn't want me drawn in. I returned a smile and a similar slow shake of the head.

An hour later the barbecue was fired up again. Along with this were mountains of bread and cheese. I asked young Fernando where the toilet was. His reply was to hold out an arm, turn full circle and say, "*El campo*." The countryside.

Lee Van Cleef pulled up in his large 4-wheel drive Toyota; I hadn't realized he had gone anywhere. He got out of the car, walked towards me, and held up a bottle of Bacardi in one hand and a pig's leg in the other. "Allaaan for you." I was desperately hoping he meant the drink and not the limb. The pig's leg, known throughout Spain as '*Jamon Serrano*', or cured ham, is to be found everywhere. It's an acquired taste that I'm slowly getting used to, much better if you remove all the fat. The leg can be left hanging for years before eating—definitely not one for the veggies.

Everybody was now on the shorts and as the drink kicked in the conversations increased in volume. When I asked what a *Hombre Festival* actually was, it was explained that one of the young men was to be married. I then realised this was the equivalent of a British stag do. As the drink and food was still being passed around I wondered who was picking up the bill. As if reading my mind, a young man appeared in front of me with what looked like a list of the names of those present. "Ten euros if you please," he said. I'd presumed that this was how today's event was to be financed. Over his shoulder I could see old Fernando giving me that same slow shake of the head. "What is it for?" I asked.

"*Las chicas*." The girls.

Now this was something else that had surprised me. Throughout Southern Spain you will often come across buildings in the middle of nowhere, or at the side of the motorway called 'Clubs'. Basically these are brothels and they are as common as McDonald's. (I must remember to explain this to the girls when they go clubbing over here.) It would appear from my young friend that it's not only the quantity that they have in common with McDonalds. The clubs also do 'take-aways'. Please notice I could have made the comparison to Kentucky's with some smutty reference to preferring leg to breast but I like to think I'm above all that.

Now I'm not sure how the divorce courts work here in Spain but handing over ten euros to this young man would surely put me on a journey to finding out.

"No, thank you." I said and Hugh shook his head to the young man, not wanting to have anything to do with it. I also noticed that the older members of the group had sloped off, obviously aware of what was coming next.

The young lad looked a little surprised. He put his hand over his eyes and said.

"You no pay, you no look."

I put one hand over my eyes and the other over my genitals and said, "Me no want anything." Finding this amusing the young man laughed and went off to share the joke with his friends. Hugh and I took this as our cue to leave and cadged a lift back to the village with somebody else who had both the age and wisdom to recognise which side of his bread was buttered.

I came home just as Heather was leaving for her meeting with the village females at the bar. "I thought you'd gone for two days," she said. When I explained my reason for the early departure she was quite taken back. Not a very good reflection on her opinion of me, I think. She was gracious enough to invite me to accompany her to the bar. We arrived to find it full of all the *Hombre Festival's* rejects, and of course some of their better halves.

One of the couples we had been speaking to the previous night introduced us to their daughter, who was up from Malaga for a couple of days. Her father had been with us at the *hombre festival* just moments before. Now he sat quietly with his wife, daughter, and son-in-law. His daughter had studied at Newcastle University in the UK and spoke perfect English—or as near as you can get with a Geordie twang.

She explained that her husband had come up for the *Hombre Festival* as he had been at school with the young man who was to be married. He glanced across and gave me a knowing smile. The daughter added, "He is allowed to go for an hour." No guesses who wore the trousers in that house. She also added, "He doesn't know where it is so my father is going to take him." As I looked across at the father, I could see a minute raise of his eyebrows and a glint in his eye. I tried to explain to the daughter that an hour wouldn't really be long enough for him to catch up with his pals and get into the spirit of the occasion, plus the actual journey takes ten minutes each way. She thought for a while, turned to her husband, and said in Spanish, "you can go for two hours." Simultaneously both the father and son-in-law gave me a wink of thanks. We never saw them again that night.

The next day the electricity company turned up and installed our meter. Power at last! Bedtime can be any damn time I like from now on. We also went down to register for gas. Nowhere in southern Spain is connected to the main gas line so everybody buys a large metal canister for about 13 Euros and this is sufficient to heat water for about a month.

We spoke to one of the locals in the bar who had a son, Ramon, who was an electrician and a plumber. (Pencil him in for Stacey). He came around and connected a water heater for us. Although we could have got this fitted before the electricity was connected, it would have been pointless because we needed the electricity to power the water pump in the garage due to the low water pressure.

Now at last it felt like it was all coming together. When I asked him how much we owed him he just shrugged and said, "*Más tarde*." Later.

Now that we had electricity I could start putting my famed DIY into action. To be honest me and DIY have never got along well together. Each Bank holiday spent in the UK would inevitably end up with me in the waiting room at the hospital's casualty department. I started by fitting a couple of mirrors that came with lights attached. The first one went up without any problems but the second one came without instructions and was a different make than the first. After a lot of cursing and improvisation it was up and looking good. Testing the lights, I flicked the switch. Nothing. I was half way through disconnecting all the wires so I could take it down and start again when Heather walked past the door. "What are you doing now?" She asked, glancing around at the mess I'd made. "It doesn't work, I'm starting again."

Heather's parting shot was, "Might help if you put bulbs in."

My only other accident (so far) was after I had put up a light fitting in the living room. Later that night I was on the floor with my back against the sofa. The next thing I knew the whole light fitting complete with 3 bulbs and shades came crashing down onto my legs. "AAARRGGHHH, Heather..... Paracetomol! NOW!"

That's why, whenever possible, I get a man in.

That night in the bar it was warm and everybody was a little subdued. I stood up and said to the small group around our table, "Watch." I pulled one of the serviettes out of the holder, waved it about and forced it into the clenched fist of my other hand. When I opened both hands and the serviette had disappeared, everybody sat up in amazement. "Again, again," they insisted. I repeated the trick and before I knew it the whole bar was watching and looking astonished. I was on a roll. I then got out a pack of playing cards and showed them another trick. I was going down a storm. Unfortunately I only know two tricks. Both these had been taught to me by Brian, a neighbour back in the UK.

The next time I went in the bar a couple of days later my audience was waiting for me, insisting I repeat the tricks. Never one to shy away from being the centre of attention, I obliged. I thought I would vary the original trick slightly this time, so I asked one of the young men smoking to step forward. I scooped up a section of his t-shirt, removed the cigarette from his mouth and dropped it, lighted end first, into the t-shirt. As I stepped back the cigarette had disappeared and the t-shirt was undamaged.

An older man had been watching on the side lines. As I refused the requests to repeat the trick he approached me and said something very quickly in heavily accented Spanish. I shook my head and said I didn't understand him. Somebody nearby who spoke a little English translated. "You are booked for the village festival at the end of June."

The next day I e-mailed Brian back in the UK. I told him to either get his arse over here for a free holiday at the end of June or post me some new tricks.

I had in my mind five ambitions that, once I had fulfilled, would make me feel like a true local.

1. Work for a day in the olive groves. (As 80% of the locals do).

2. Drive a tractor.

3. Play the locals in a domino competition.

4. Speak Spanish like a local.

And the fifth may take a little longer.

5. Become Mayor, or *El Presidente* as it is called in the village.

My first was to come to fruition quicker than I thought. Fernando, as well as owning the bar and the local home for *Hombre Festivals*, also owns an olive grove. I happened to mention that I wouldn't mind helping out one day and the next thing I knew he had offered to pick me up at 7am the next morning.

At 6.15am I was up and dressed and eager to get to work. The car horn blew outside and the two Fernandos sat waiting. One was in a small Renault that I found out later was thirty-two years old and looked like that was the last time it had been cleaned, both inside and out. The other was in a Land Rover about the same age.

A little while later I was being instructed in my duties. The olives had been picked, so my job was to rake the debris, old leaves, and branches from beneath the trees, scoop them into a large bucket and tip that into the waiting trailer. I was working alongside young Fernando because the bucket was quite heavy when full. Heather and I had often driven alongside the olive groves and commented how back breaking the work looked. I can now categorically confirm that it is.

On one occasion young Fernando had to move the trailer closer to where we were working. As I had filled a bucket on my own I thought I would carry it by myself just this once. Struggling toward the trailer, my foot went down a rabbit hole, and I went over on my ankle and dropped the lot. The pain was excruciating. I could see old Fernando smiling and shaking his head. "Okay?" he asked.

Sí," I replied with my bottom lip quivering and a tear in my eye. I got up and continued.

Throughout the day as the trailer filled, young Fernando and I would make the short ride to the olive factory and dump our waste into the cruncher. During one visit he asked if I would like to drive the old Land Rover back. I agreed. He then asked if I would move it back, whilst he signed the paperwork in the office. "*No Problema*," I said. Having once owned a new Range Rover, how difficult can it be? I jumped in, closed the door, started the engine, and reversed it back about twenty feet. He seemed to be a while so I turned the engine off. Well, I turned the key but the engine continued. I removed the key but still the engine ticked over. As Fernando returned I showed him the key and asked how you stop the engine. He said nothing, just pointed to a big sign in red letters that said "Pull lever to stop engine." It was even in English. I felt so small I wasn't sure I could reach the pedals any more.

With the key back in and the engine started once again, we set off down the narrow lane back to where we were working. I felt completely in control. I now know there is a difference between being and feeling in control. As we came to the first bend I turned the wheel ever so slightly to the left, but the vehicle didn't move. I turned a bit more—nothing. By now we were drifting slightly off the track so I turned the wheel a little more aggresivly. The car bucked to the left and started going up the embankment. It was clear by now that the steering had a ridiculous amount of play. It was possible to turn one way and the vehicle would go the other.

Young Fernando found my wrestling with the steering wheel highly amusing. The smile was wiped from his face, as around the corner, coming head on, was an old tractor. "Stop slowly!" he shouted. I remember thinking at the time that was bad English, surely he means "Stop quickly!" No, he was correct; what he had meant was brake gradually. As I put the slightest touch on the brake pedal the breaks locked and off we went into a prolonged skid. Of course trying to steer clear was not really an option, not only because the lane was extremely narrow, but also, as I had learned, the steering had a mind of its own. We stopped with inches or, should I say, centimetres to spare. Oh how Fernando enjoyed retelling the tale to his father. I later found out that the Land Rover hadn't been serviced for twelve years, had no MOT, tax, or insurance.

"*Sólo para el campo.*" No need, only for the countryside, had been the reply from young Fernando when I asked.

My ankle still ached like hell. At 12 o'clock we sat in the middle of the field and had a spot of lunch. We were supposed to be finishing at 2pm but as we were doing so well it was suggested we fill one more trailer. At 3.30pm we all agreed we had done enough. "Just a minute," I said. "Part of the agreement was I would get to ride a tractor." I was hoping to fulfil two from my wish list on the same day. Old Fernando apologised and explained that his brother was using the tractor that day. "Never mind," I said. I had brought my camera; in fact, I take it everywhere. I set it up on a timer to take a picture of all three of us leaning on the trailer. (Fernando's copy is still up behind the bar).

I staggered into the house and collapsed onto a chair. "How was it?" Heather asked.

"Never again. *Primero tiempo y ultimo tiempo.*" First time and last time.

E-MAIL

FROM Ashlie

Hi mum and dad.

Thank you for the Birthday card how did you know where we'd be?

I woke to my room filled with balloons and opened the pressys that Stacey had got me...... the tattoo of flowers on my hip was my main one. We spent the day by the pool and in the afternoon went to see a chic flick. At nighttime we went round the bars. Stacey kept telling them it was my birthday so we blagged loads of free drink. On one occasion we had a tequila cocktail...... love cocktails..... hate tequila!! Stacey made me drink it all.

We met up with a lad we have been sharing a room with at the hostel, so ended up in an Irish bar with him and his mates. They all got up on to the bar and did pole dancing. The lad we knew was Scottish and had his kilt on...... I'll leave that to your imagination mum. All we'll say is he got us all a $60 free bar tab.

Love you both.

Ash xxx

Heather wasn't happy about the tattoo. "It could have been worse," I suggested. "Just think, if instead of flowers she could have had the words, *I like it down under.*" Heather didn't even smile.

Chapter 9
What a Boar

It wasn't uncommon for me and Heather to take a long walk after tea. In fact, most people regardless of age can be seen at different times of the day strolling along roads and country lanes. I was told that if you go to the doctor with an ailment the remedy prescribed is usually given as a 'distance to walk' each day. That was one reason why I kept my swollen ankle to myself.

On one of our after tea strolls we went a little further than we had expected and ended up cutting across the fields as the sun went down. The next day we were talking to Hugh and Sylvia outside Lee Van Cleef's house when he brought out a couple of stuffed animal heads and hung them on his outside wall. "What's he doing with those?" I asked.

"He's putting them outside while he paints the front room," Hugh answered.

"I don't mean what's he doing with them I mean why has he got them?" The heads were gross, about the size of a horse's head covered in dark-brown, course hair with sharp teeth and pointed tusks facing upwards on either side of the mouth. "He hunts them, last month they had a 'drive' down the valley and they shot seventeen of them."

"You mean those things roam around out there?" I pointed over my shoulder into the countryside.

"Yes. They're wild boar, but you're okay, they normally only come out at night time." My mind drifted back to me and Heather clambering around the night before as it was getting dark. I couldn't miss this photo opportunity. I went home, collected my camera, and knocked on Van Cleef's door. When I asked if I could have a picture taken with his trophies to e-mail home to my friends he was delighted.

"*Un momento*," he said and dashed back indoors. Five minutes later he returned with all his hunting paraphernalia. Another five minutes later he was photographing me standing under the heads of the wild boar wearing a hunting jacket, matching hat, and two shotguns in my hands. When I sent the e-mail to my friends in the UK I put under it the caption:

ME, TAKING IN THE WILD LIFE.........OR SHOULD I SAY TAKING OUT THE WILD LIFE.

As I left, Van Cleef invited me to take part in the hunt next November.

The bar, if you had not already gathered, is the centre of village social life, as it is in most villages anywhere in the world. I had never had a pub I could call my local, a bar you can go into any day at any time and know there would be somebody to have a chat with. That was until I came to Spain.

When we walk into the village bar the first couple of minutes are usually taken up with greetings from the people already in, and throughout the night greetings are extended to and from the people who come in afterwards. Our regular visits to the bar had enabled us to become friendly with a group from the village. I was going to say a family from the village, but this would have been less than accurate, because we later found out that just about everybody in the village is related to everybody else in one way or another.

The locals are so generous that we found ourselves inundated with free drinks. Quite often at the end of the evening when we came to settle our bill, we would find that it was the equivalent of only one or two drinks, even though we had been in the bar all evening. This was because people would just ask the person serving to move some of our bill onto theirs. Others would walk past our table and put down a drink they had bought for us, smile and walk off. Some would think this Utopia but to be honest it made me feel very guilty; none of the locals were particular wealthy, or so I thought, and many would be up at dawn to go to work, whilst I would sleep in and do virtually nothing all day. To get around this, as soon as I went in to the bar I would get a round of drinks in, for anybody and everybody who I thought might buy me one.

One evening we decided to go to the next village to check out the bars there. I joked with Heather that at least we wouldn't have the problem of everyone trying to either pay our bill or ply us with drink. I ordered a couple of small beers and took them to the table. When we had finished and agreed to move on, I went to settle our bill. "No need," said the barman and he nodded to the end of the bar. Standing there, smiling, was the owner of 'Pepe's', the bar in our village where Heather felt uncomfortable and used to hide *tapas* in her handbag.

You may wonder why people don't just pay for their drinks when they buy them; well that's not how it's done in Spain, certainly not in the mountains. You don't settle your bar bill until the end of the night. Usually the barman will keep a running tab behind the bar and tot it up at the end. Quite often though, in the bar in our village, he will just ask what you have had and pick a figure out of thin air. Another one you just can't imagine catching on in the UK. " Honest gov. hic. I've only had two, hic, Cokes all night."

On some occasions, like when Real Madrid football team are playing live on TV, the bar can get quite busy. When this happens it's not unusual for the person serving to be overworked. I have in the past ordered a 'usual' (Bacardi and Coke), and the bar tender has just passed me the bottle to help myself.

Now settled in our home with water and electricity, we decided to redeem the family pets from the cattery. On our way back to the UK a few weeks earlier, we had called in to see them. The owner of the cattery, Nigel, was a Brit who had lived in Spain for twelve years. He greeted us at his front gate with, "Are yer scared of dogs?" As he said this he was joined by a large Alsatian on a long chain. Heather hesitated. "It's okay, he's chained up, he can't go

74

anywhere," Nigel added. The last time I heard that phrase was in the *King Kong* film and we all know how that turned out.

The dog's curiosity lapsed and he returned to his kennel to finish the bone he'd been chewing on when we arrived. The owner opened the gate and in we went. We crossed the yard and came to another gate. Beyond were four Dobermans all quietly staring at us. "It's okay, they have been fed," said Nigel in a voice that hid if he was joking or not. "Back!" he shouted, and as one they all bounded off to a small outhouse and went inside. Nigel followed them and closed the door. Once again we followed him across the courtyard and into a large barn. Inside were five large cages, each one containing a contented feline—except for ours. Digby and Ollie shared a slightly larger cage than the others and both looked as miserable as sin. It took a while for them to recognise us but when they did it was plain to see they were overjoyed.

Now, almost a month later, we rang Nigel and told him we were ready to have the cats back. "No problem," he said, "but it would be better if you could call in rather than me delivering them," he added with a nervous voice.

"That's not a problem," I said. Then curiosity got the better of me. "But why?" I asked.

"The black one is a vicious little bugger, she's had me a couple of times and now I can't get her out of the cage without her going for me." Is this the same person? I thought. The man who orders Dobermans and Alsatians around, scared of little Ollie? We had agreed later that day would be a good time to retrieve them, and off we went.

Once again it took a while for them to recognise us and, true enough, Ollie did need a little coaxing from the back of the cage, but an hour later we were at our new home. Pamela had said that whilst she had looked after them Digby had spent most of the time meowing, including throughout the night. As Digby explored his new home he began the meowing that would haunt us for the next two weeks. The fact that the house had little furniture and the floors were tiled gave any sound a slight echo, and Digby's voice was no exception. As he picked up on this he tried to do different noises, almost experimenting, from a high-pitched shrill to a deep growl. The effect was quite comical.

After a couple of days Heather and I agreed that the time had come to let the cats out of the house and let them go exploring. That night, as I was going to bed, I remembered that I hadn't fed them. Even though we had electricity we had no bulb in the kitchen so, in the dark, I rummaged around looking for the dry cat food. Eventually I found it and put a handful in the small terracotta dish the cats used.

When I got up the next morning I let both Digby and Ollie out. Wearily they left the garden and disappeared into the olive groves. They didn't come home that night.

Heather was beginning to panic. "Did you feed them before you let them out?" she asked.

"I fed them last night." Heather went over to the untouched food dish.

"No bloody wonder they haven't come back!" I looked into the dish to see that what I had put out for them the night before, in the dark, was cat litter.

"I'll go and find them." I spent the next two hours walking through the countryside shouting their names, convinced we would never see them again. I could just imagine Digby's shrills and growls translating to "If this is what the Spanish pass for cat food, I'm off!" Eventually I found Digby sitting forlornly under an olive tree looking all sorry for himself. I took him home to find Ollie waiting on the terrace for the both of us, wiping the tuna off her face, obviously a present from Heather. Somehow I had a vision that that should have been my tea.

When I have previously referred to the 'kitchen' I may have been exaggerating slightly. Yes, the room was intended to be a kitchen, but at the moment it was just a tiled, empty room. No cooker, units, sink, or anything. We had to go and order everything. So off we went to a town called Lucena, about a one hour drive away. Why so far? I hear you ask. Well, apparently this town is made up of furniture factories, and anybody and everybody buys all their furniture from there. Now can you imagine trying to order a kitchen in a foreign language? There's sizes, quality, colours, appliances, etc, etc. A veritable minefield of problems. But after finding somebody that spoke as much English as I do Spanish we just about cracked it. We were told a man would come around to do the final measuring up and after that it would take 4 or 5 days...or was it 45 days?

The man turned up a week later with his tape measure and began sizing up our requirements. Now I wasn't sure if it was a nervous tick or just a reflection on the builder of our house, but every time he measured something and wrote it down, he would shake his head and tut loudly. When he'd finished he asked for a ten percent deposit. I asked him how long it would take and he said about 45 days. That answered my earlier question. So for the next month and a half the tiny camping stove would be the centre of our culinary creativity.

E-MAIL
FROM Stacey
Thanks for my birthday card I would love to know how you get them to us.

Ashlie got me a fantastic birthday present. I thought she was just taking us to a dolphin show but she had actually paid for us to be trainers for the day. We were shown how to feed them, train them to do tricks and even swam with them.

We are going out for a drink tonight to celebrate.... Oh yes, I nearly forgot. Yesterday Ashlie and me were sat on a bench and two Chinese men came and sat next to us, they wouldn't leave us alone. They said they would pay us a lot of money to spend the night with them, so to get rid of them I agreed and told them a false room number in a hotel I could see in the distance...... somebody's going to get a shock tonight!

Speak soon
Stacey xxx

Chapter 10
A Wedding with a Difference

A wedding invitation was brought to the door addressed to:
Don Alan y Hemguer
Unfortunately none of the Spanish can spell or pronounce 'Heather'. The wedding was to be between one of Lee Van Cleef's sons and the daughter of the brother of the person we bought the house from. Come on, keep up.

The Scottish couple, Hugh and Sylvia, had also been invited, and as Sylvia had been to a wedding the previous year we asked her what the form was. Apparently with regards to presents, the tradition is simply to put into an envelope what you think you are costing. For example, if you think the meal and what you are going to drink comes to €50, then that is how much you contribute. It's damn easier than going down a wedding list where nothing on it is under £200.

During a discussion with the groom's mother, she asked me how an English wedding differs to that of a Spanish one. I explained how, for Dutch courage, it's not unusual for the groom and some of the guests to partake of a beverage, even before the service. She frowned and made me swear that I would not turn up drunk. I agreed and then reflected on the low opinion she has of me. Sylvia had also mentioned that the previous year she had turned up to a village wedding dressed to the nines, including hat, to find that the other villagers had gone in aprons, overalls, and even dressing gowns, changing only for the reception afterwards. I checked this with the groom's mother and she insisted that we dress up and attend the formal service down in the town.

The big day arrived and, wearing suits, Hugh and I, accompanied by our better halves, made our way to the church. Sylvia had offered to drive. We parked the car and walked the short distance to the church. Outside we found the groom and the rest of the family and friends eagerly awaiting the bride.

In the distance we could hear the sound of car horns being held down. This, I'm told, is a warning that the bride is on her way; nobody moved an inch. I suggested that we should be taking our seats but after a short debate we thought we had better take our cue from the rest of the people outside the church.

The bride's car pulled up, horn still blowing. As well as the guests, a large number of tourists had stopped to take pictures. She hooked her arm into that of her betrothed and went inside. A few minutes later they were followed by just a few of the guests.

We thought it unusual that the happy couple enter first, but even more unusual was that by the time we got in, the priest had already started the service. As he continued, over the next ten minutes the rest of the congregation strolled in, and thought nothing about shouting across to people asking how they were. This we found very strange. To be honest I anticipated a long, drawn out, formal service.

Now you expect the official wedding photographer to be moving about, taking pictures and checking the lighting, etc. What I didn't expect was the rest of the congregation to start strolling around during the service with cameras and videos clicking and whirling all over the place. I counted at least five people walking up behind the priest, placing a camera just over his shoulder, and snapping merrily away at the happy couple. Out of the corner of my eye I noticed a middle-aged man holding a white handkerchief to his mouth. He then appeared to be trying to shove it all the way in, and he seemed quite frustrated by something. As he removed the handkerchief, I realised that the pallet of his false teeth had come out over his top lip, and he was trying to rectify this quite ghoulish site without success. After another five minutes of trying, he pushed his way to the end of the pew and disappeared out of the church.

The service came to an end and the newlyweds walked hand in hand down the aisle. By now, as well as guests milling about, tourists had entered and walked around looking up at statues and paintings as if it was an open day.

The bride and groom waited at the main door for all the guests to pass them and go outside to await the grand exit. As is custom in the UK, people were poised with bags of rice and confetti, and in addition to this many were holding bags of nuts. At first I presumed these were to eat but as the happy couple came out, as well as the rice and confetti the nuts were thrown as well. The problem was some of these were almonds and walnuts, still in their shells and about two inches across. The wedding photographer clicked away but instead of pictures that would provide an everlasting memory when developed, these would show the groom doubled over the bride as both of them tried to shield themselves and each other from the flying debris. The crowd outside all found this hysterical.

The wedding had started at 5pm and the reception was to be held at a large hotel on the outskirts of town at 9pm. To kill a couple of hours, I, Heather, Hugh, and Sylvia went to a local bar to begin the night's festivity.

Arriving at the hotel just before 9pm, we were led into a large dining hall that already contained some of the guests from the church. I'm not sure what I was expecting but I must admit I was pretty impressed. The room was decked out for the occasion and there was adequate seating for over five hundred guests. I noticed that it was only a third full. I asked Lee Van Cleef, the groom's father, "Why all the empty seats?" Before he had time to answer, hundreds of people piled in the side door. It was the rest of the village; a number of coaches had been laid on to bus them all down to the reception. Now the place was full to capacity.

The four of us joined a table that already had three couples sitting down, only one of which we had spoken to before. Sitting down, we introduced ourselves to the other two couples. Hugh whispered to me, "I'm glad I didn't get sat next to happy." As I scanned the table I realised he referred to one of the wives sitting opposite. She was staring straight ahead with a stern expression, speaking and apparently listening to nobody. Visually she was the double of the character played by Les Dawson, the large-breasted woman who looked over each shoulder and adjusted her bosom before passing on gossip to her friend, played by Roy Barraclough.

The meal consisted of five courses and bearing in mind that none of the Spanish present spoke English, we all seemed to be getting on fine. Well, I say that none of them spoke English but that wasn't entirely true. Halfway through the second course one of the women said, "I am speaking of the little English." This is going to be interesting, I thought. "I am knowing only some few words." It was refreshing to find somebody who was at least willing to give it a go, so I asked her where she had studied. "I am remembering from at school." Bearing in mind that this woman was about sixty years old, she must have had a damn good memory.

She was on a roll now and playing up to her appreciative audience. She placed her finger on the side of her lip and looked upwards trying to conjure another few words from her distant past. "I like piss!" she said.

The English speakers at the table went silent and were taken back by this announcement. "Pardon?" I asked. The woman sat up in her seat and declared with gusto, "I like piss!" Trying not to smile, Heather, Hugh, Sylvia, and I all looked at each other; none of us dared to open our mouths in case we burst out laughing. The woman was looking at us, waiting for some kind of response; she must have read our expression of bewilderment because she stabbed her fork into the salmon on her plate and repeated again. "I like piss!"

"Ah," I said, "Fish," with great relief.

"*Si*, Piss!"

During the meal, trolleys were forever circulating, stacked high with every kind of drink you can imagine—wine, beer, soft drinks, bottled water, etc. All this was free and by the fifth course spirits were high. A group of young men from the village began gathering at the head table. Our dining companion, who likes piss, became quite excited and pointed to the small crowd. This was obviously one of their traditions, maybe the speeches?

The young men, chanting and cheered on by the guests, carried the groom from his seat around to the front of the Head table. They then removed his trousers, putting his tight fitting Y fronts on show for everybody. It didn't stop there. These were skilfully removed using a pair of sharp scissors and placed on a silver tray. By now we could all see what his new wife was going to be getting for supper, and I don't think she was going to be disappointed.

A bunch of young women then, a little more gracefully, escorted the bride to the front of the main table. Hugh and I gave each other a knowing grin. I had noticed how Heather and Sylvia had enjoyed the groom's participation and now it was our turn. Alas she simply pulled up her wedding dress and allowed them to cut the garter from around her thigh, and this too was placed on the silver tray.

I would have loved to see Heather's mother's face if this had happened at our wedding. To my astonishment these two articles were then cut up into small pieces and offered for sale, and all the pieces were eventually replaced with Euro notes.

Ten minutes later the younger guests once again approached the head table, only this time they were carrying 2 cakes. These were a little less ostentatious than the 5- tiered one that sat to one side. These in fact had been expertly modelled into the shape of a woman's and a man's private parts, the coloured icing giving them startling realism. The male version was placed in front of the bride and the female's in front of the groom. As the onlookers cheered, the bride's and groom's heads were pushed into their respective finely modelled privates.

A little later, one of the young men asked me to show his friend from another village the trick with the disappearing cigarette. I obliged and by the time I finished a small crowd had gathered and applauded the outcome. Lee Van Cleef patted me on the back and gestured for me to go around with my hand out. "I don't understand." I asked him to explain. What he said in Spanish was "You have entertained them so go around and collect some money for yourself." I couldn't believe he actually expected me to go around with a cap for donations; he didn't understand when I refused.

By 12pm everybody had moved into the adjacent room. In there they had the disco and the 'shorts' bar well, to be honest all they had was whiskey or Baileys. If earlier spirits were high, then by now they were truly through the roof. I was glad to see that even though we were over a thousand miles from the UK it was still tradition to make a complete prat of yourself at a wedding disco, shirts were un-tucked, ties were off, and all inhibitions had been deposited at the door.

Hugh, being a true Scot, was knocking the whiskey back like water and not to be out-done, I was pathetically trying to match him glass for glass. This went on until about 2am when it was suggested that we, the remaining twenty or so, go clubbing. In fact I have a vague recollection that it was me who made the suggestion. And before you say anything, I meant clubbing UK style, not the local brothel.

By 7am I had just about danced myself into the record books and had probably made quite a reputation for myself, as what I dare not imagine. Even Hugh was beginning to look a little unsteady on his feet, although he was convinced that it was the fact he was tired and not the twenty plus drinks we had downed. Somebody shouted, *"Desayuno,"* which I knew translated in English to 'Breakfast'. Everybody cheered in agreement. I looked at Heather through bleary eyes and with slurred speech declared, "Thank God for that. I'm ready for my bed."

Nobody was going home; we were all going on to a hotel/bar that served breakfast.

The menu was pretty limited. In fact, the only thing placed in front of me was some bread and a piece of cured ham. Hugh ordered a beer and that's when I threw in the towel. I could keep up with him no longer and resorted to a nice cup of coffee. We arrived back home at 8.00am, went to bed and slept the rest of that day.

E-MAIL
FROM Stacey/Ashlie
Hi folks
Well, we have gradually worked our way right up the east coast of Australia and arrived at Cairnes. To be honest we are a little disappointed. We were going to stay here for a while and look for jobs but we have decided to head back down to Brisbane and find work there.

We have heard that the best and cheapest way to get down to Brisbane is to go to a mobile home company that needs one of its vehicles driving down. They don't pay much but at least we don't have to pay them.

Will let you know how we get on.
Stacey and Ash xxx

A couple of weeks later our kitchen turned up. It was then I was informed that in Spain the fitters don't actually connect the sink to the pipes or the electric cooker to the electric. We would need Ramon, our friendly plumber/electrician, again. The fitters popped their heads around the corner to say they had finished; I followed them into the kitchen to inspect the work. "Just a minute," I said, "where are the work surfaces?"

"There is coming in two days. Different company," was the reply.

Fair enough, two days later the worktops were on and that same night Ramon called in to connect the appliances. An hour and a half later he had connected the sink and the oven but had found the hob to be damaged when he removed it from the packaging.

As he left I asked him how much we owed him including what was outstanding from fitting the boiler. "You pay when all is finished," he said. This worried me slightly because I normally like to settle up as I'm going on, except for in the bar of course.

A phone call to the kitchen company resulted in us making a choice: we either go all the way to Lucena and have it replaced the next day, or wait a week or two until they had a van in our area. We decided to make the two-hour journey rather than wait.

Once again, Ramon called around and spent another hour beavering away. Heather and I discussed how much his bill was likely to be. "He's done about four and a half hours altogether," Heather said.

"Yes but he's had to come out three or four times so there will be call out charges. Plus the materials." I tried to tot it all up in my head. There were pipes, special taps for the gas and water fitments, a flue, and some sealant. I estimated the bill to be about 350 Euros (£240). Heather thought it would be much more.

After Ramon had finished he escorted me into the kitchen and explained the workings of the cooker, fortunately as the instruction booklet was only in Spanish. "Very good," I said smiling and using the Spanish I had been practising awaiting this day. "And how much do we owe you for everything?" He looked a little embarrassed then muttered something. I only caught the first number but knew it began with a nine. *"¿Qué?"* I asked him to repeat himself, hoping I hadn't heard nine hundred.

"Noventa." He said, again looking a little unsure of himself. I was wrong, he hadn't asked for nine hundred, he had asked for just ninety Euros. For coming out four times and working for over four hours, including parts, he was charging the equivalent of £60. I gave him a hundred Euros and when he put his hand in his pocket for change I told him that it wasn't necessary. He was overjoyed.

Chapter 11
Our First Visitor

We had often e-mailed our friends and told them that they were all welcome to come and stay with us. I think it may have been the snippets I included in the beginning, like we have no water and electricity, that resulted in only one person taking us up on the offer.

Pamela, Heather's sister, arrived at Malaga airport the following Sunday. We looked forward to her visit especially as she was the first of many, we hoped. Heather and I had prepared a full week of entertainment, starting the next day with a village shindig in *el campo* (countryside).

Lee Van Cleef had asked me to meet him to help load the tables and chairs onto the back of a trailer. A breakdown in communications meant that by the time I had arrived the job had already been done, but the beer still had to be loaded. He asked me to follow him to Fernando's bar. The bar was closed but the door was ajar and in we went. Van Cleef made his way behind the deserted bar and started filling crates with beer bottles from the fridge. He passed these to me and I put them on the waiting trailer. When I returned he was holding up a couple of bottles of Bacardi and several of whiskey. After passing these to me he scanned the rest of the optics to see what was available. After several more trips to the trailer it crossed my mind that I may just be part of a robbery. If I was going to go down then I would have rather taken my chance at the Notary with the supermarket bags full of cash, at least the rewards were greater.

Fernando appeared at the door. I looked up, by now I had a crate of red wine under each arm. "*Hola*," I stuttered. He crossed the room slowly and relieved me of my swag; he then left the bar and placed them on to the back of the trailer with the rest of the drinks.

Out in the *campo*, preparations were underway. The barbeque was burning brightly and not with charcoals from the local supermarket—no, they just break bits off nearby trees and shove them on. I remember cancelling a barbeque back in the UK because I didn't have any charcoals or briquettes, how pathetic that seems now.

To one side the *paella* was also well underway, and each time I see one of these creations it appears bigger than the last. At a long table the women were preparing salad. It's funny how most women do the cooking indoors but once outdoors and over a naked flame the men all suddenly turn into Jamie Oliver.

The drink we had collected earlier was all placed into a large barrel of cold water and throughout the rest of the afternoon, regardless of how much was drunk, the volume never seemed to go down. As the various meats were deemed ready on the barbeque, a plate would be filled and brought to the table. Each time I would point and ask what kind it was. This would result in everybody within ear shot of the question imitating the sounds of the various animals, and not only the sounds but some people would also put hands on their heads with index fingers pointing upwards and either hop about or scratch the ground with one foot. It was amusing when the pork was served. Without even asking, several of the women sitting near me wrinkled their noses and grunted with heads bowed down. It was so tempting to pretend not to know which animal it was, just to prolong the entertainment.

Once the food had been dispensed, the men congregated around a large table and out came the dominos. Not knowing the intricate variation to the rules that the Spanish have, I remained at the long table with the women. And what game do you think appeared from nowhere? Yes you've guessed it. Bingo.

For the next hour or so I joined in playing until the woman calling the numbers became bored and a replacement couldn't be found. "I'll do it," I said. All the magic markers that were being placed back in the handbags suddenly remerged. I wasn't too bad and made some mistakes, but they were patient and found my calling as amusing as I had found their animal impressions.

Sitting to one side was a very large man in a uniform drinking beer. "Who is he?" I asked. Van Cleef explained that he is the local countryside ranger and it was his job to make sure that the fires were under control and that on departure we cleared up after ourselves. He seemed to be taking little interest in the proceedings except, that is, for the barrel containing the alcohol. "Isn't that his car?" I enquired, pointing to a green Land Rover with a deer on the side and a small fire burning underneath. The fire cooking the *paella* had crept across the dry grass. Van Cleef shouted, "*Pepe!*" and nodded toward his car. The ranger tutted, strolled across to his car and kicked some dirt at the fire, eventually it went out and he returned to the drinks barrel.

By now everybody had been drinking for about four hours. Pamela leaned over and whispered. "Where's the toilet?" When I had asked this same question at the *Hombre Festival* a young man had waved his arm around and said, "*El campo.*"

So I did the same to Pamela. Within minutes she was shuffling up a small path looking for a bit of privacy. We saw her dip behind a large rock but then jump up again as a couple of the kids from the village ran onto the top of it. She shuffled a little further up the hill and stood behind an olive tree. This also gave insufficient cover so off she went even further. Heather and I were watching with curiosity. "If she goes any further she might as well have gone back to the village," I said, wondering what I'd do when the time comes. Eventually she returned. "Why so far?" I asked.

"Oh I wanted to get a photograph from the top of the hill."....Yer right.

It began to get dark so we all cleared up and returned to the village. Just as we were leaving, Fernando came across and invited us to another gathering in the *campo* the following week. "What's the occasion?" I asked, knowing damn well that an excuse wasn't needed. I still couldn't make out his Andalucian accent but his son explained that it was the end of the olive season, and as I had helped out I was considered part of the family. In the short time that we had been here I was beginning to feel more accepted than I could have possibly hoped for.

E-MAIL
FROM Stacey/Ashlie
Hi
Well we made it. We found a place that wanted a campervan taking down to Brisbane although it was a bit of a rush we did the 1065 miles in three days. I must admit that it was a little different to drive than the Fiat Saxo I had.

During our mini road trip we managed, when making popcorn in the microwave, to burn a plastic bowl and my finger . . . spill wine all over the cushions. Stacey tried to attach a hose pipe to a tap, when she turned it on, it sprayed in every direction . . . soaking everything.

When we arrived in Brisbane we found a hostel in a magazine and booked in there. We think it might actually be some kind of mental institute! It's full of old people and we feel quite privileged that they let us out on our own.

Tomorrow we are going on the ultimate bush tucker trial... Agghhh! You get Kangaroo, Croc and Emu but at least it's cheap.

This weekend is Buddha's birthday. Stacey and me thought it was somebody in our group but apparently it's a religious thing.

Will speak soon.
Stacey and Ash xxx

Although rain is a rare commodity in southern Spain, it must have known that Pamela was here. As a sun worshipper she didn't seem to share the locals enthusiasm for the downpour that lasted the next three days, which was torrential. We didn't let it dampen our enthusiasm or interrupt the visits we had arranged; we donned our coats and off we went. When the rain did eventually stop, Pam covered herself in suntan lotion, laid out on the sun lounger, and she was as happy as a pig in s**t.

By the end of her holiday Pamela had fallen in love with our lifestyle to the extent that on her return home she was talking about opening a B&B near us. Well, it couldn't be any worse than Maureen and Joe's...or could it, doll?

In the UK Heather would normally get her hair cut at least once a month, but it had now not been cut for nearly six months. Her vanity would also insist that she dye it every two or three weeks as well. This wasn't a problem whilst living on the coast because the brand of hair dye that she used back home was available in the local shops. Unfortunately it wasn't where we lived now.

Heather returned from doing the weekly supermarket shopping on her own one day. "What's this?" I asked, removing a box from one of the bags.

"Hair dye," she replied. When I looked at the box a bit closer I noticed that it said *RUBIO*. "Why have you bought blonde, you normally go for brown?" Heather spun around. "It's not blonde. The picture on the box is a woman with brown hair." I didn't argue.

The next day Heather came out of the bathroom having just used the new dye. I said nothing and just smiled pleasantly. The result wasn't too bad, but for the rest of the day, every time I looked at her I couldn't help but hum the tune to, 'The Tide Is High.'

This wasn't the first time Heather had struggled with the language so it was agreed that she would enrol at Spanish classes down in Loja, the local town. Unfortunately she only attended for a few weeks. The majority of what they were teaching was the basic grammar and Heather wanted to concentrate more on conversation.

Not long after we had moved into our new house we realised that if you were out on the terrace and the patio door closed then you would truly be stuck. The terrace to the front was built over a double garage and the only way on and off was via the patio doors into the house. There was another option, a twenty-foot drop. Once we realised this we had made a pact that when we are both on the terrace you never close the patio doors.

One night as I sat on the terrace, Heather brought me out a sandwich . . . and she then closed the door behind her. Fortunately, at the time of the pact we also made a back up plan, by hiding a spare front door key in the garden. There was just the matter of the twenty-foot drop to over come. As I teetered on the edge I asked Heather if she would help me by lifting my right leg onto the side. I am hoping that there was no malice intended and she simply misheard me, because she lifted my foot and literally threw it over the edge.

I sat on the floor nursing my scraped arm while Heather looked down on me and said, "Look at the mark you made on the wall as you went down." She was serious. Nevertheless our back up plan had worked and the spare key enabled me to rescue my damsel in distress; though, after her so-called assistance, I was in two minds about leaving her up there for a while.

Now you would imagine that once you have made a mistake that resulted in a minor injury that you wouldn't repeat it. Alas, two weeks later the only difference was that it was I carrying the food this time, but yet again that unmistakeable sound of a sliding door shutting was right behind me. I cringed at the thought of going over that wall again; heights have never been my speciality.

This time I refrained from asking for assistance and levered myself into the abyss. I scraped my arm on the way down and landed with the finesse of a cat with no legs. Heather's head appeared above me. "You've done it again, look at that mark." I was too busy looking at the graze on my arm, not the skin I had deposited on the wall.

Plan 'B', the hidden front door key, had not allowed for somebody leaving a key in the lock on the inside of the house, and as we didn't have a plan 'C' we were well and truly stuffed. I explained the situation to Heather. She replied, "Although the blind is nearly all the way down on the bedroom window I think the window behind it is open." This was obviously Heather's plan 'C'. I looked up at the bedroom window. "Even if I could open the blind from the outside, how the hell am I going to get up there?"

"You need a ladder!" she said stating the obvious.

"Where am I going to get a ladder?" I asked a little impatiently. Heather nodded into the distance behind me. When I turned around I realised she was meaning the building site where they were halfway through building half a dozen new houses. "But I only have my socks on." Her reply was to simply shrug her shoulders. So off I went. I trod carefully over the stones and general debris you expect to find on a building site, only to find it deserted of workmen. I was just about to leave when I heard a noise from one of the garages. I went a bit further to find all the builders on the floor chatting away and having their sandwiches. "*Hola*," I said gingerly. They stopped and eyed me up and down. When their eyes got to my feet they just stared. The first thought I had was, how the hell am I going to explain my predicament with my limited Spanish? "*Mi casa, no tengo una llave.*" (My house, I have no key.) "*Necesito . . .*" I didn't know the word for ladders so I held my hands out as if I was holding the rails and lifted my feet alternately. One of the workers turned to his colleagues and said, "*Inglés.*"

"Ah," they replied in unison as if that explained everything.

Five minutes later I had hobbled back to my humble abode, ladder over my left shoulder. I rested it against the terrace and climbed up. I then pulled the ladder up onto the terrace and leaned it against the house wall. It was then that I noticed all the builders had come out of the garage to watch, so I gave them a cheery wave.

The ladder was a little short but I managed to pull myself up onto the railing of the bedroom balcony, a quick vault and I was over. I turned around expecting applause but my audience seemed less than impressed. The blind blocking my entrance had been designed to be opened and closed via a pulley system on the inside, and if I couldn't open it I wasn't sure I could get back down to the ladder. This could be highly embarrassing.

I cupped my hands underneath it and heaved; it hardly moved at all. Glancing over my shoulder I found I still had everybody's attention. I bent my knees and put my back into it. It lifted about ten inches and would move no further. There was nothing else for it, I would have to try and keep it up and at the same time try and slide underneath it. I decided for some reason that it would be better to enter feet first, why? I have no idea. Halfway through the blind dropped and pinned me down. This was more embarrassing than just being stuck on the balcony. I must have been there for several minutes. I glanced in the direction of the building site. The workers were too far away to be heard but I'm sure I could see their shoulders going up and down. I placed my hands on the ground beneath my chest and gave an almighty shove, and the blind lifted only an inch, but that inch was sufficient to enable me to complete my slide underneath and into the bedroom. Once in, I lifted the blind completely, stepped out onto the balcony, and took a bow. The workers drifted back to their garage, disappointment all over their faces.

Now we do what we should have done in the first place; we block the door with something every time we come out.

I have always been a fussy eater ever since I was a child. In fact, during my youth my diet consisted mainly of fish fingers. My mother tells me at the age of six she took me to the doctor to find out why. I suppose now they would just make a T.V. programme about it. He asked if I ate bread and sweets, etc. "Yes," she replied.

"Well then, he doesn't only eat fish fingers then, does he?" was his answer. " He'll grow out of it," he added as she left.

Alas, he was wrong and my diet is still very limited. I only eat vegetables raw, but I eat most meats. Heather jokes that I don't eat anything warm that isn't brown or beige. This, you can imagine, causes some problems when friends invite us over for dinner; I even ask if I can vet the menu before it's chosen.

I have tried to be a little more adventurous since we moved to Spain, but I do on the odd occasion have to draw the line. A good example of this was when one of the locals brought a dish of snails into the bar, put them out onto several plates, and placed one in front of Heather and I. We looked at each other with eyes that said, "you first." Even Heather, who normally tries anything, said no to these.

A man facing us misread our hesitation and thought that the problem was that we just didn't know how to eat them. He used a small stick to dig one out of its shell and held it out for me to take straight into my mouth. I could have sworn I saw the snail wink at me as a show of appreciation when I refused the offer. Unfortunately, the man threw his head back and dropped it straight down his own throat, so the reprieve was short lived.

The next night I heard the same woman that had brought in the snails explain that her husband was next door cooking some 'Pájaros'.

"Mmm," They all replied with vigour.

"What are those?" Heather whispered.

"I don't know," I replied, "but I guess we are going to find out."

At this, her husband came into the bar with Van Cleef. They ordered a jug of beer and turned to leave. "Allaaan," shouted Van Cleef from the door. He held up the beer and said, "*Para los pájaros*," and signalled for me to follow him.

The building next door was a large white house that I later found out was owned by the woman who produced the snails the previous night. I followed Van Cleef and the woman's husband, a retired policeman, through the house to the kitchen. "I thought you lived opposite the church," I asked the ex-cop. He then went on to explain that this was his other house. How many houses do these people own?

In the kitchen on the cooker was a large pan. Van Cleef slowly poured in the beer as he stirred. "What are they?" I asked. Before I had finished the sentence a small bird with feathers missing was lifted from the pan. The bird was about the size of a sparrow and was only one of about twenty being stirred and sprinkled with seasoning.

When the meal was deemed ready, the pan was carried back into the bar. Once again a plate was placed in front of Heather and I. The plate contained three shrivelled fledglings with bits of pepper clinging to their tiny bodies. Everybody else was diving in, ripping the young bodies apart with their fingers and devouring each morsel with relish. "I suppose it's only like eating chicken," I suggested, unconvincingly.

Heather picked one of the birds up and gently removed a piece of flesh from under the wing; she bit into it gingerly. "Not too bad," she said as though she was trying to convince herself more than me. I followed her lead and lifted the smallest of our featherless friends from the plate. I was just about to take a bite when I noticed a part of it I didn't recognise. "What's this long bit with the lump on?" A Spanish woman sitting to my right saw me examining the bit in question. "*La cabeza*," the head, she said, and then shoved the same part of the bird she was holding into her mouth. She pulled at it until the head was separated from the body by her front teeth. I placed the bird I was holding gently back on to my plate. "I think I'll stick to the crisps and nuts in the future."

In passing I happened to mention to the others gathered at our table that Loja, our nearest town, had come into the 21st century, and now had a Chinese restaurant. I was expecting the usual, "It's all cats and dogs they serve." What I wasn't expecting was when one of them said, "I saw a programme about those restaurants. Did you know there are 2 million Chinese live in Spain... and nobody's ever been to one of their funerals." The rest of the people, who sat nearby listening intensely, all gave a mutter of agreement.

A few days later, Heather and I went down to Loja to try out the new restaurant. When we returned to the bar the following night, I announced to the table that Van Cleef headed, "We've just tried out the Chinese restaurant." A large intake of breath was taken by all who listened, I think a few of them crossed themselves and muttered a few Hail Marys. "What did you eat?" asked Van Cleef.

"I had the fried rice with a plumber, Heather had a deep fried solicitor." I then went on swiftly to explain that I was joking.

Things were moving at a pace now. A visit to the local 'telefónica' shop and our phone line was ordered. After typing in our details, the girl behind the counter announced that it would all happen in—now did she say 4 or 5 days, or 45 days? Déjà vu!

It took some chasing but eventually a telephone line was connected, and we even had Internet. During a conversation with another English couple, Jim and Diane, we happened to mention that we had just had a telephone line put in.

"Don't mention telephones to me. We've been trying for nearly 2 years to get one and have been told that we can't have one because our house is more that 100 metres from the nearest house with a connection." She was getting quite hot under the collar now. "I even wrote to the town hall in Loja to complain," she added.

"What did they say?" I asked sympathetically.

"2 men turned up and erected a telephone post right outside my front door. I was so pleased I went and got them both a bottle of beer. 10 minutes later when I went back out they had gone. I waited a week for somebody to connect the wires and when nobody came I rang the telephone company."

"And?" I asked as she stopped for breath.

"They had no record of any poles being put up."

"So what did you do?" I asked

"I've written to Brussels, to see if they can't get it sorted." I thought this rather drastic but to my amazement Diane got a reply from a Euro MP who said he'd look into it for her. A month later she had her phone.

Not long after the telephone line came the 'English' T.V. Compared to everything else, getting this was a walk in the park. We phoned a number advertising 'SKY' in the free paper from the coast, and the very next day an overtly gay chap came and fitted a satellite dish to the side of our house. When I queried about the size, he told me that the one he'd fitted was the smallest available to do the job. It was massive, so if I ever get bored with *Coronation Street* I'm sure with a simple twist of the TV tuner I'll be able to chat with the space station.

Chapter 12
In the Summer Time

Summer has arrived in Spain with temperatures reaching 45 degrees in the shade. Heather sat watching *Calendar*, the local news station back in the UK. The weather forecast was for heavy rain over Leeds, our former home in what seemed a former life. "Can Ollie, Digby, and I go back to England for some lovely rain?" We hadn't seen any for 3 months.

With summer comes the real fiesta season. It started last Sunday with our neighbouring village, Balerma, having theirs once again in the middle of an olive grove. This time everybody brings their own table, chairs, and BBQs, and throughout the day you are entertained with everything from horse races to the local priest blessing everyone.

Heather and I were sitting under an old tree watching a choir of 6, accompanied by a sole guitarist singing traditional songs. Two of the singers wore white masks; I later found out that quite a few people are badly affected by the pollen from various trees, and in fact, at this time of year a dusting of yellow covers almost everything.

A couple of women emerged from a clump of trees that had been designated '*los servicios*' or toilets, wandered over and asked if we would like to join them, at the same time nodding toward two men wrestling with an out of control barbecue. "We noticed the car registration." Over my shoulder the glaring yellow of my British number plate was like a beacon in comparison to all the other white Spanish ones.

We introduced ourselves and soon found our hosts to be Carol and Bernie, who lived in Balerma and were at the time accompanied by some friends from the UK. We moved our chairs across to join them and thus began a friendship that still thrives today.

The afternoon moved into evening and as the strength of the sun waned I spotted a few of the young lads from our village preparing a horse for the race that was to be the last event of the day. Though I had never ridden a horse, I was not one to miss a photo opportunity. I strolled nonchalantly over and asked if I could sit on it.

"*Sí*," replied one of them as he cupped his hand to help me up. Once aboard, the young scallywag (not what I called him at the time) slapped the horse's rear, and that was me off for a tour of the olive groves and anywhere else my trusty stead decided to explore.

30 minutes later and the horse had gotten bored, or I had gained control, I'll never know which. We emerged from the trees and rejoined the festivities. The young lads from earlier were still giggling like little girls. "Sorry Allaaan, I am thinking you can ride."

"Yes sure," I smiled as I handed him the reins, to show there were no hard feelings.

Back in the UK, Scott (Ashlie's boyfriend) had the operation he had been waiting for on his knee. The next day he got his ticket and flew out to meet up with the girls in Australia to join them for the rest of their journey. I'm sure the hospital wouldn't have agreed with him taking such a long flight, but love clouds so many judgements. Having told him to let us know when he'd arrived, we received the following e-mail.

E-MAIL
FROM Stacey/Ashlie
We've met up with Scott, you should see the size of his leg!

As poor Scot has to sit there while we watch soaps on an evening we thought we would surprise him and get us all some tickets to see the Broncos Vs Tigers rugby match.

We entered Suncorpe Stadium to join the 31,500 fans and found our seats. We didn't know a thing about rugby and Scot had warned us that he didn't want the game spoiling with us asking questions every two minutes.

As soon as the game started I (Stacey) had a question! Scott's reply was to stand up and point at me whilst shouting at the top of his voice. "This girl has a question, would anybody care to answer it!" I could have died. Ashlie and me weren't the only ones not interested in the game. Throughout the afternoon the man sitting next to me spent all his time looking at the cheerleaders through his binoculars.

After the game we went to a proper barbecue, not like yours dad where everybody waits an hour for you to light it, then all scramble at once for the only cindered sausage. No, this was like a real sit down meal with everything ready at the same time.

Got to go the bus is waiting for us.

Stace, Ash and Scott x

Ps Can't tell you what we are doing at the weekend. . . . You wouldn't approve.

I wish they wouldn't do this to me!

Everything seemed to be coming together with the house so we thought we'd take the plunge and try and get the swimming pool put in. (Did you like the play on words there?) We wanted to give the work to somebody from the village and were recommended a builder, Manuel, by Hugh and Sylvia. He came to the house to discuss our requirements, but it became immediately apparent that we had a language problem. Manuel's Andalucian accent was so strong that most of the words were unintelligible, except for the few English words he knew—then the problem was his Scottish accent. Manuel had become quite good friends with Hugh, or Hugo as the locals renamed him, and his curiosity with the English language had resulted in a few lessons from Hugh. Manuel's greetings would often be, "Yer allreet?" and on departure he would call, "Al be seein yer!"

Hugh once told me of an occasion where he and Sylvia had looked after Manuel's two small children whilst he and his wife attended the overnight vigil of his Uncle's coffin, something the whole family does at the funeral directors. Manuel had asked Hugh to drop the children off at the funeral directors at 8am the next morning. Hugh said when he arrived there was nobody outside so he went in. He was greeted by the mourners who sat around the coffin that contained the late Uncle— who by the way was in a sitting up position. Of course the atmosphere was very solemn, that was until Manuel stood up at the back and with a Glaswegian accent matched only by Taggart himself, announced, "Hugo, there's beeeen a murrrderr!

Anyway back to the pool. Manuel and I were making little headway, so rather exasperatedly he slammed down his pad and pen and stormed off. Ten minutes later he returned with Emma, Hugh's daughter. Although she is only 12, in the year that she had been here she has mastered the language like only a young mind can, and she speaks like a local, including the overt use of the hands and the excessive shrugging of the shoulders. Many of the building terms were beyond her vocabulary but her help made a difficult job a lot easier. So with notes, measurements, and sketches in hand, Manuel toddled of to make his calculations. "Al be seein yer!" He called as he slipped through the gate.

A couple of days later Manuel came by to present his findings. The quote was about €18,000 for a tiled pool with filter, pump, and the surrounding garden made into a patio. Each item had been priced up individually, from the rental of the JCB, to the cost of the tiles. We showed him that a pool had been on the original plans so he came up with a completion date of 4 weeks hence.

Alas, after further investigation, I found out that although a pool was on the original drawings of the house, it hadn't been included in the planning permission. "No problem," I thought. How hard could it be? I'll just take the original drawings to the town hall and ask for the permission.

So off I went the next morning. A short conversation with the woman at the main desk resulted in me being passed on to a smart, middle-aged man behind a computer terminal. I proudly showed him my original planning permission for the house and explained that I now wanted permission to build a pool. His accent was soft and clear, so for once I was having a conversation in Spanish without having to say *"¿qué?"* or *"¿cómo?"* every 2 minutes.

The man asked if I had a quote from the builder I intended to use, and without hesitation I passed him the formal quote from

Manuel. "*Muy bien*," said the man as he played the computer keyboard like a concert pianist. Seconds later the printer behind him buzzed into life and ejected an official looking document. He passed it to me with the words, "*1650 Euros por favor.*"

I looked at him blankly and out popped the word, "*¿Qué?*"

A friend had told me that just because the pool was on the original drawings it wasn't full blown planning permission that I required, just an amendment. Not so. I waffled for a minute, apologised to the man, and said I would return later.

On the way back to the village I bumped into Manuel and relayed the story to him.

He took a deep breath, went as white as a sheet, and mumbled something to the effect of, "Tell me you didn't show them my quote."

"Yes. Why?" He then went on to explain how things are done over here. Apparently the cost of planning permission is a percentage of the work to be carried out; therefore you are supposed to take to the town hall a quote that actually represents about a quarter of the original one.

"Oops," I said, with a Spanish shrug of the shoulders.

"Tomorrow we will go to the town hall together," said Manuel with a sigh.

The next day Manuel and I (Heather didn't fancy getting involved in illegal activities for some reason) marched into the *Ayuntimiento*, Town Hall, and once again we were directed toward the smart man behind the computer. I didn't catch what Manuel said, but a few nods in my direction accompanied with a few choice words that Van Cleef normally reserves for me when I cock up, told me that I was taking the blame for this. The final word, "*inglés*," seemed to explain everything and once again the keyboard was played and the printer buzzed. "*185 Euros por favor*," said the man as he passed over the permission to go ahead.

On the way back to the village I asked Manuel what he had said, and he explained that he told the official I was a bit slack and had brought the wrong quote. For a saving of €1465 Manuel could spend all day calling me whatever he likes.

A week later I walked up the garden to watch Paco, the JCB driver, turn over the first sod. Let me correct that; I have looked once again at Manuel's quote and this could in fact be the second sod that's being turned over. After 10 minutes I hobbled back into the house. "Why are you walking like that?" asked Heather.

"I don't know, over the last couple of days my foot has started hurting, especially my big toe." I presumed I must have twisted it, or even been bitten by something.

That night in bed the pain was excruciating. I couldn't even stand the weight of the bed sheet on my toe. During the night Heather got up to go to the toilet. As she past the end of the bed she banged against my foot.

"AAARRGGGGHHHHHH!!!" I screamed

"Tut," she said, "you do exaggerate," she muttered as she carried on her way.

The next morning I searched the house high and low for painkillers, but to no avail. "We'll have to go down to Loja, can you do the driving?" I suggested to Heather, whose sympathy hadn't increased much from the previous night.

Hobbling to the car I saw Van Cleef coming down the road. *"¿Qué es el problema?"* What's the problem? he asked.

"I don't know," I replied, "I have this pain in my foot and toe but I don't remember injuring it."

He smiled, "I know what that is," he said.

I frowned. "What?"

"Gota."

A quick flick through the dictionary in the car and there was the translation. GOUT! "Didn't that die out with the plague and only affect fat old men that do nothing but lay around all day eating and drinking?" His raised eyebrows spoke volumes. "I'm going to the *farmacia* for some pain killers," I added, dropping into the passenger seat.

"Ask the chemist," Van Cleef shouted over his shoulder as a parting shot.

In Spain the chemists are a little different than back in the UK. People will often go to them for advice with minor injuries and illnesses instead of the doctor. At the *farmacia* I asked for the Paracetomol and mentioned, almost in passing, the pain in my foot. After a short pause I added, a little embarrassed, "My friend thinks I may have gout."

"Then you need a blood test," suggested the chemist. "Come back here tomorrow at 1:30."

After another restless night Heather and I returned to Loja and entered the *farmacia*. The chemist suggested I take a seat and wait. Outside, a car pulled up and the driver got out. He put on a white coat, entered the *farmacia*, smiled, and asked me to follow him into a small office. He introduced himself, read the note the chemist gave him, and proceeded to take a sample of my blood. When he'd finished I asked, "When will the results be ready?" Thinking back to the National Health Service I expected the answer to be a couple of weeks.

"This afternoon," came the answer. This was impressive but it did cross my mind to wonder, how much was this going to cost?

Later that day I returned and the chemist presented me with the results on a printed sheet. The report was unsurprisingly in Spanish and showed the result as percentages of this and that. The chemist, recognising my confusion, took the sheet from my hand and glanced under his spectacles at it. As he passed it back he announced. "You have gout; take this to your doctor." At the time this meant nothing to me, as I had no idea what the illness entailed. One thing that did go through my mind was that Van Cleef is in the wrong job.

"How much do I owe for the test?"

"4 Euros," (£2.80) said the chemist. How do they do it? I thought, counting out the change.

Driving back through the village, I saw Van Cleef strolling down the road and asked Heather to pull up along side him. "*Hola*. The chemist said it was gout, how did you know what it was?"

"What you described," he said. "Exactly the same as Fernando at the bar, he's had it for years."

I went to see the doctor who visits the village twice a week. Alas, her heavily accented Spanish made her explanation of the condition difficult to understand, so I accepted the prescription she offered and resigned myself to do my own research on the Internet.

Back home I brought up 'Google' and typed in: LIVING WITH GOUT. The porn site titled 'Down on the farm' was a bit of a surprise, then I realised I had typed: LIVING WITH GOAT. After correcting my mistake I eventually came up with an informative medical site that told me gout is the result of having too much of a certain acid in your blood, which eventually crystallises in the joints.

The article went on to say that "Attacks can be reduced by removing the following from your diet: All alcohol, especially beer and wine, red meat, fish, poultry, eggs, food cooked in oil, nuts, some vegetables, etc, etc." Oh yes, I also have to drink between 6-8 pints of water a day. So I am left with a choice; I either carry on as normal and walk with a limp and a cringe, or I live the life of a Buddhist monk on a retreat to Outer Mongolia.

I wonder if I can get a walking stick on the Spanish National Health?

My ability to withstand pain was tested again a couple of weeks later. Some friends, Allan and Denise, had popped over from the UK for a short trip. Their arrival coincided with the finishing of the pool. Well, I may be slightly exaggerating. The pool was finished but it was in the middle of what looked like a building site. Around the pool was an unprotected 3ft ditch. I had just finished warning our guests to be careful when—yes, you know what's coming—down I went. Heather's usual female instinct prevailed; she burst out laughing, along with Alan and Denise.

I began to pull myself out. "AAAAARRGGGGHH!" I yelled. As I had slipped down, one of the reinforced spikes had gone into the side of my leg. I didn't cry but I must admit my bottom lip was shaking like a shitting dog. When I eventually got out, the laughing died down and we examined the wound to find a deep hole, no blood, but it was weeping profusely. The ladies put a plaster over the hole, and not wanting to upset our dinner arrangements, we all disappeared and got ready to go to Granada.

An hour later whilst walking from the car to the restaurant, Denise pointed out that my injury was now leaking onto the outside of my trousers. "You need to have that looked at," said Heather. Across the road I noticed a *farmacia* still open and after my previous success in Loja I decided to call upon their services once again.

Once inside, I explained my predicament and the chemist gave me some Iodine, a packet of swabs and a couple of large plasters. I asked if I could deal with it in the corner of the shop, and that's what we did. Heather, with an evil grin, soaked a swab and bent forward to go to work. At this point a woman crossed the shop, took the swab from her, put even more Iodine on and went to work, pushing her finger into the hole in my leg. After I had climbed down from the roof she taped another swab to my wound, stood up, picked up a shopping bag and walked out... She was just another shopper!

E-MAIL
FROM Stace/Ashlie/Scott
Sorry I couldn't tell you what we were doing but I have put some pictures in the post. I can defiantly say BUNGEE JUMPING is the scariest thing ever. Ashlie bottled out so me and Scott did it . . . in fact we had three goes each!
Moving on to New Zealand in a couple of days
Bye
Stacey Ashlie and Scott.x

A couple of days later we sat with Van Cleef and his wife Encarna, and the conversation got onto the subject of food once again. "Rabbit is my favourite," confessed Van Cleef.

"I've never had rabbit," admitted Heather.

"*Mi casa, domingo próximo.*" Van Cleef's invitation to Sunday dinner will have been the first time we have eaten with a proper Spanish family in their own home. It was something we looked forward to with mixed emotions.

Not knowing Spanish etiquette for such an occasion, we dressed casually and, before leaving the house, selected a bottle of wine to take. "I've just remembered. Encarna doesn't drink and Van Cleef only drinks whiskey," said Heather, so I swapped the bottle of wine for one of whiskey.

During the short walk to their house, Heather and I mulled over the possible menu.

"He said it was going to be rabbit," I pointed out.

"I'm just thinking back to the bar when they were all eating sparrows and snails," Heather said nervously, her nose curling a little.

"We have to eat whatever they put in front of us," I said, "it would be rude not to."

We knocked on the door and were greeted by Van Cleef himself. I passed him the bottle of whiskey. He looked at me, then the bottle, then back at me. His expression said, "You have a drink problem my friend." Inside the house it was quite dark, as most Spanish houses are. Alfonso, Van Cleef's son, was engrossed in a cartoon on the T.V. and seemed to be finding it hysterical, a little unusual when you consider he is 19 years old.

We took our positions at the table and right on cue in walked Encarna, carrying individual plates full of assorted vegetables and…some kind of animal. Heather and I glanced at each other recalling our vow to eat, or at least try, whatever was put in front of us.

Now I know this was to be Heather's first taste of rabbit but I just don't ever remember seeing a rabbit with wings, so presumably some kind of last minute substitution had been made. We all picked up our knives and forks and began to dig in. Encarna saw me pushing the meat around, got up and disappeared in to the kitchen. When she returned she passed me a pair of scissors. "What the hell are these for?" I whispered to Heather. Across the table from me, Alfonso had rejected the knife and fork and was pulling the animal on his plate apart with his fingers, so I did likewise. The wing looked tempting so I gave it a tug. It came away from the body. Unfortunately where it had been joined hung the veins and tendons, still dripping with blood and bodily fluids.

"*Antonio, ¿no conejo?*" Not rabbit? I asked.

"*No,*" he replied. He then stood up, hooked his thumbs under his armpits and waved his elbows up and down. From this I deduced he was either trying to tell me we were eating bird, or we had progressed on to charades and this was his Dick Van Dyke in *Mary Poppins*.

Heather, who had been sitting at the side of me throughout the meal, let out a faint squeal that fortunately only I heard. As I turned my head I saw her pulling something from her mouth. Was it a bone? A bit of gristle maybe? Or even a filling? No, it was a piece of buck shot the size of a small rock. "I guess he shot it himself," I said.

After the main course, a bowl of fruit was brought from the kitchen, and Heather selected a pear and took her first bite. "*No, No,*" called Encarna thrusting a knife toward Heather. "I think she wanted the pear," I said a little worried. As it transpires, the knife was to peel the pear, as they never eat the skins of fruits, concerned about what they may have been sprayed with.

As we said our goodbyes I returned the invitation and promised that next time they would have to come to our house for a meal. Van Cleef turned his nose up and curled his top lip. A rough translation of what he said would be. "I don't think so, I don't eat that English muck."

Just like anybody else, now and again we need a holiday. So when Heather's sister Anne texted us to say she and her husband Adey, along with their son Mark and his girlfriend Lucy, were all holidaying in Portugal, it didn't take us long to load the car and set off.

420km later we had arrived. As the apartment had only 2 bedrooms, we got the sofa bed, but when you remember that only a short time ago we were sleeping on cold tiles with no electricity and water, it was pure luxury.

We had decided to act like any other British holidaymaker and spend all our time drinking, eating, and cavorting, just for a change. The gout had not troubled me for some time, so fingers crossed it was a one off, probably brought on by dehydration, as I was told is possible.

The weather was just what you would have expected; it rained constantly for 2 days—on one occasion right in the middle of the England game (World Cup), and we were watching it outside at the time. A Scottish man at the next table stood up and put his right hand on his heart, as the national anthem was played for England's opponents, Ecuador. He looked across at me and said, tauntingly, "I should learn this."

I called back. "You might as well; you never need to sing the Scottish one."

On the last day we started drinking whilst watching football in the afternoon and finished up downtown in a bar going through the cocktail menu. We agreed at 2am that it was home time but missed the small sightseeing train that was to take us home.

"No problem, there is another in 20 minutes," said Anne. So to kill the time we nipped into another bar. Throughout the day I had had a couple of drinks spilled down me so when it happened again in the last bar I wasn't sure whether to order a short or sit in a corner and suck my jeans.

The barman reluctantly obliged our request for music and suddenly we all turned into contestants for disco dance champion

2007. We were all jiving away to Bill Haley when I turned in Lucy's direction, bent my knees and slapped my thighs. She immediately recognised the invitation to run and jump at me with legs apart.

Now I know Lucy won't take offence when I describe her as curvaceous with over-developed breasts. But at the instant she began her run I felt my life pass before my eyes. She ran like a chased gazelle, left the ground, and hit me with full force. At that exact moment I knew what a pin feels like at 'LA BOWL'. Her chest hit me full in the face and almost broke my nose. She clung to me like a limpet as my weak ankles buckled. After swaying back and forward for a few seconds I slowly went forward like a felled oak. The landing was ungraceful and thank God she was wearing underwear beneath her dress. At least she cushioned my fall.

The trip home on the mini train developed into mayhem when, for no reason at all, we all broke into song. The song? 'Doe a Deer' from *The Sound of Music*, don't ask why because I have no idea. All I can say is that if like the Von Trapp's we had to rely on our vocal skills to escape the Nazis, then the gas chambers would have been our next stop.

Walking toward the apartment we were greeted with a large prostitute bent over, leaning into a car window, wearing a very short skirt and no underwear. As we approached, she walked off with the driver.

Anne and Adey have a tradition; every night is finished off with a pint of Bailey's and ice... each. We decided to have this on the balcony. This was when we noticed another scantily clad female in the same car getting up to shenanigans with a man with 4 arms. No, my mistake, his friend in the back seat was joining in. Pure class.

Toward the end of the holiday, the sun came out and we all decided to spend the day on the beach. When we returned to the hotel in the late afternoon I seemed to have sand in every orifice of my body. I suggested it might be a good idea to have a swim in the hotel pool, rather than have everybody trail the sand into the apartment. So that's what we did. I did a couple of lengths, then just before I got out I went to a discreet corner of the pool, pulled down my trunks, and got rid of any sand remaining. Returning to the others, all lying on sun loungers trying to dry themselves in the sun, I dropped onto one of the beds and commented what a nice large pool the hotel had.

"It is quite a posh hotel," Anne said, "in the reception area there is a window that shows you under the water of the pool."

"Which part of the pool does it show you?" somehow I knew what the answer was going to be.

"That corner over there," she said pointing to where I'd just come from. I gathered up my things. "I think I'll go and get a shower," I said making a tactful exit.

When we returned home the first thing I did was to check our e-mails.

E-MAIL
FROM Stacey/Ashlie/Scott
Hi again.

On the plane to New Zealand we managed to get the seats at the front, it was like being in 1st class with all the legroom. Once up in the air a sign appeared on the screen in front of us, it read "Thank you for not smoking." Then we realised this was the beginning of the in-flight movie and that's what it was called. What will they show on the way back? 'Please remain in your seats'

The airport in New Zealand was really strict and we had to declare all our wooden objects we had brought over from Australia A guy spent ages looking at our didgeridoos and after getting 2nd then 3rd opinion he told us that he would let us keep them if he wrapped them up, and we didn't open them until we were out of New Zealand. Thank god, there was no way we had carried half a tree trunk each around with us for 5 months, only for some airport guy to take them off of us!!!!

Got something special planned but can't tell you.

Speak soon. Stacey, Ashlie and Scott x

Chapter 13
San Juan

Back at the village an air of excitement was evident as everybody prepared for the San Juan fiesta. Throughout the next week a variety of competitions are held, everything from football to darts, dominos to tennis. Although I'm not very good at it, I put my name down for the darts.

Heather announced, "I want to play dominoes." A few of the men in the bar frowned and shook their heads. One of them muttered, "Women don't enter the dominoes." At this, and quite surprisingly, Van Cleef came to Heather's defence. "Let her enter if she wants." I'm sure I saw him give the men a sly wink. One of the other women sitting nearby, rallied by the revolt, called out, "I will partner her."

The next night, I played my first game of darts. I won. Heather waited for her partner, who didn't turn up. "Perhaps she'd just been carried away by the moment," I suggested. "More likely by her husband," Heather lamented.

"I'll be your partner," I volunteered. The two lads who were to be our competition sat opposite and looked quietly confident, in fact even more so when Heather posed the question, "So how do you play then?" We had both played the game back in the UK but assumed the rules to be different in Spain.

As it turned out, the only differences were that they play counterclockwise, score slightly differently, and slam the pieces down in an effort to intimidate the competition. Or so they said. I later found out that when a domino is slammed down on the end of a line, it is a signal to one's partner that he (or she) doesn't have any of those numbers left.

The game began with more than a few onlookers, and to the frustration of our adversaries, we were winning. The Spanish are passionate about most things, but if you ever get a chance to watch a game of dominoes, you'd think they had bet all their worldly belongings on each lay of the tile.

Forty-five minutes later, Heather and I were declared the winners. The two young men stood up and slinked out the back door without saying a word, unlike the onlookers who laughed and jeered them for getting beat by amateurs.

The next night was to be the second round of dominoes. I walked up to the board in the bar to check the fixtures. "Oh my God, Heather, you won't believe who we are up against! Van Cleef and Paco." I mentioned earlier the passion that dominoes create in the most sedate Spaniard. Well I have watched these two play before; they spend half the time shouting at each other.

Whilst waiting for them to turn up I played my next round of darts. I was as surprised as anybody when I won.

A shove in the back and some choice words in Spanish told me that Van Cleef had arrived, and we took our places. "In this game no speaking English," Paco announced.

I smiled at Heather. "I think they believe we only won last time because we were telling each other what we had in English." I turned to face Paco. "*Sí, no inglés y no español,*" I said in an effort to even the playing field.

Fifteen minutes into the game and we were winning. By now a crowd had gathered to watch the impending defeat of the favourites, Paco and Van Cleef, not us. The no talking rule went out of the window. As each domino was laid, either Paco or Van Cleef would fire a volley of obscenities at the other. However, as soon as Heather or I opened our mouths we were told to shut up in no uncertain terms.

The best way to describe the atmosphere would be... the scene in *Deer Hunter*, where the hero was forced to play Russian roulette? The Vietnamese crowded around the table while the gun was raised slowly, sweat ran down the participants' backs while the perspiration beaded through the bandanas on their foreheads.

CLICK.....Nothing. Cheers of relief and disappointment rocked the small room while glasses shook and beverages sloshed over the rims. Now, substitute the click of the gun with the slam of ivory and ebony dominoes and you're halfway there.

Alas, fate wasn't with us on this occasion and the victory went to the other side, but I think we scored a few brownie points with the locals for giving it a go.

"Allaaan!" called young Fernando. "It is you for the next round of the *diana*." I presumed this meant darts. I had noticed that each round I played, I had for some reason become quite nervous about playing. I have no idea why.

My first few throws I believe reflected this, so I brought my Bacardi and Coke over to the table near the board and took a deep swig. To my and my opponent's amazement, all the darts went in the bull, and as this was what I needed to end the game. Victory was mine. I was through to yet another round.

The next night, halfway through watching a film, the doorbell rang. *"¡Venga Allaaan... diana!"* Apparently I should have been in the bar playing the next round of darts. Heather and I refused the offer of a lift on the young man's motorbike and walked to the bar. After another Bacardi to settle my nerves, and on top of some wine whilst watching TV, I felt a little tipsy. What the hell, I thought, it didn't do any harm last time.

Now I'm not sure if it was luck, the god of all things pointed, or simply the drink, but I couldn't do a thing wrong. My darts were like mini exocets. The crowd watched in awe. (Am I over egging the cake here?) And a bull! Game to ALLLLLAAANNN!

I was actually through to the final. Could it be possible? No, surely not.

Another Bacardi, and once again, my little arrows hit the mark every time. Somehow my opponent and I had hit all the required numbers. The bull was the only one left. The adjudicator announced that Juan (my rival for the cup) needed 3x bulls. He then called out that I needed 5. Was this some sort of foreigners' handicap system? Nevertheless I continued. A few minutes later through my intoxicated blur everybody in the bar was patting my back and congratulating me, I was to be the first foreigner to take to the stage of *primeros* at the end of the fiesta. I raised my hands and declared myself the champion. *"¡Champiñon!"* I shouted. The laughter that surrounded me broke the atmosphere a little. It was then that I remembered that Spanish for champion is *'campeon'*. Apparently I had just declared myself as the village...MUSHROOM!

The booklet with the timetable for the long awaited village fiesta said everything would commence with a fireworks display at 8am Friday.

At 7:50am Heather and I walked into the centre of the village, but there wasn't another soul in sight. Everything was set up, the outside bar, the dodgem cars, etc, but nobody was there. At 5 past 8 we bumped into another English couple, Jim and Diane, and they too were wandering aimlessly, looking to the skies in anticipation of the signal that would start the 3 days of celebration, only to be disappointed.

We agreed that we hadn't misread the programme and eventually decided to go to Pepe's bar for a coffee. Already sitting there was one of the locals nursing a hangover.

"Where's the fireworks?" I asked.

"The organisers are in bed, too many beers last night," he replied.

"So, when will the firework display start?" He shrugged his shoulders in reply. That's the timetable for the bin! I thought.

An hour later a man walked into the square holding 4 rockets. One at a time he held them out, lit them with his cigarette and waited for launch. After the last one departed, he left. "Some firework display," I said. The rest of the day's events were all on a similar scale, which made me wonder why the fiesta had been talked about so much and built up for so long. Later I found out.

That night the stage came alive with a 12-piece group, 8 of which were singers, 4 of whom were scantily clad young females. The drink flowed and everybody danced. We were seated at a table that was mostly taken up by Van Cleef and Encarna's family.

"Allaaan," shouted Van Cleef, which for some inexplicable reason always makes me feel nervous when he says it. For the next ten minutes he explained this brilliant idea he'd had. Tomorrow evening we will go around the tables. You perform magic and I will hold the hat and collect the money. *"Cinquenta/cinquenta,"*

50/50 he said, like he was doing me a favour. The celebrations finished at about 6am and we all retired to our beds.

The next night of the fiesta was a little more sedate than the previous night, partly because everybody was completely knackered. "Can we have Marie and her troop on stage please," announced the compere.

"That's the girl who took step class," says Heather. A couple of months ago a step class was advertised in the village. Heather, a big fan of this style of exercise back in the UK, went along to investigate. When she returned I asked, "How did it go then, is it going to be a regular thing?"

"No!" barked Heather, "Everybody else was about 11 years old, the music didn't work properly, and afterwards I felt like I had hardly done anything." Although Marie, the teacher, asked Heather each time she saw her if she would be coming the following week, Heather always seemed to have a good excuse, but at least all the kids said hello each time they saw her.

Anyway back to the fiesta. Marie took her place on stage followed by 10 youngsters. They all positioned themselves and Marie started the music. "Oh my God!" said Heather. We turned and asked what the problem was. "That is the class I took and they are doing the same routine. If I had carried on going I would have been up there with them." We all agreed that between us we would have paid heavily to see that performance.

"She turned too early," commented Heather with just a little too much knowledge for an innocent observer. I wonder if it's too late for Heather to get one of those black leotards with the red sash. Mmmmm.

"Thank you once again to Marie's dance troop," announced the compere. "Next we have the presentation of the *primeros* (competition winners) and after that I am informed that Allaaan, Ventorros De La Laguna's top magician, will be taking to the stage to perform just for us."

My heart sank. I thought Van Cleef and I were just going to be doing the odd table for a couple of Euros. From in front of the stage Van Cleef winked at me. I nodded and smiled back whilst under my breath I spoke the words, "I'll get you, you little shit."

The presentations were made and of course I responded to the call "Allaaan" and went up for my darts trophy. I was also given a plastic bag that contained a shirt, quite a nice one actually, and Heather's kind words of support, "Could have done with being a size bigger," did nothing to tarnish my moment of glory.

The presentations came to an end and I was introduced. On reflection, being introduced as the village's best magician isn't as prestigious as it sounds, since I was the only magician! Because most of the tricks I had prepared were card tricks I placed a table in front of the stage and waited for people to gather. Nobody came. I was dying before I had started.

Eventually a small crowd gathered and I began my repertoire. (I had increased it from the 2 tricks that I knew earlier by buying a book on simple magic.) In fact the crowd became so large I had to get on the stage so everybody could see. So up I jumped and with one or two willing helpers, I was going down a storm.

Although there were probably a couple of hundred people, not one of them noticed my sleight of hand. I was hamming it up and milking it for all that it was worth. I must point out that at this stage my audience hadn't seen much magic before and were perhaps not the quickest of what Spain has to offer; in fact, if there had been an eclipse due I could probably have got away with incorporating it into my act. Forget that, I'm not sure what they do with witches and warlocks over here.

After leaving the stage, Van Cleef dragged me to the bar and filled my trophy with Bacardi and Coke. I'd laid off the drink until then... I'm a professional I'll have you know. I changed (at the request of the '*Presidente*') into my prize shirt, a black one, and made a few more cigarettes and coins disappear. God, I even looked like David Blain now.

At about 4:30am the music stopped and the crowd dwindled. Back at the table with Van Cleef's clan I held my head in my hands and said, "Thank God this is the last night. It will take me a month to catch up on my sleep."

"*Próxima semana hay la fiesta de comida*," said Encarna.

I nudged Heather, "We have to do it all again next Saturday. Apparently it's the 'food fiesta', whatever that is." One thing you can't fail to notice living in Spain is that all the villages are either completely deserted, due to everybody having siestas or just escaping from the sun's rays, or everybody is out in the squares partying. It seems to go from one extreme to the other. It's all just fiestas and siestas.

During the week it was explained to us that the '*Fiesta de comida*' is where all the women in the village produce a delicacy in the kitchen at home, then bring it to the awaiting tables in the plaza at 10pm. "What am I going to make?" asked Heather. We decided to ask the advice of somebody who had been there and done it, so to speak. So off we went to visit Carol and Bernie.

"It's a very important event," advised Carol, "everybody makes some food at home, and at about 9:30pm you take it to the village square. Everybody will be looking at what you take."

"No pressure then," I said.

"What the hell am I supposed to make?" asked Heather, thinking back to the time we invited Van Cleef and Encarna back to ours for a meal. "I don't eat that English muck," he had replied.

"I've got a great idea," said Carol disappearing from the room. A couple of minutes later she returned holding a 10 inch jelly mould in the shape of a penis.

"They will think it's so funny, I got this from Anne Summers. You could make a pink one and a brown one." I was just about to laugh when I realised she was deadly serious. "Thanks," I said, accepting the plastic penis.

The journey home was mostly carried out in silence. Heather, holding the mould out between thumb and forefinger as though it was some kind of prosthesis, said, "I don't think...."

"No, neither do I," I said, knowing what she was thinking.

Our eventual offering was to be cornflakes covered in chocolate alongside pears filled with tuna. I bet you had to read that twice didn't you? Yes, it does sound a funny concoction but the chocolate corn flakes we thought would appeal to the kids, and the pears filled with tuna was something we'd had at a friends house, and do in fact taste gorgeous.

As a joke I did make a jelly using the mould Carol lent us and popped it in the fridge. When Javier, one of the young lads in the village called, as he often did, I said, "Do you want to see what we are taking to the *Fiesta de comida* tomorrow?"

"*Sí*," he said. I went over to the fridge and brought out the jelly penis.

"What do you think?" I asked trying to keep a straight face.

His eyebrows went up in surprise, and then down in to a frown, his lips started to form a word then thought better of it. His expression said, "How the hell do I talk him out of this one?"

"*Sólo una broma*," only a joke I said. The relief was written all over his face.

The following night we carried our culinary delights to the plaza and were greeted by Paco, the domino player. He tended to take charge on occasions like this. In front of us were two tables that ran the length of the square. "That one is for main course and the other is for desserts. Which do you have?" Now I must admit that this question foxed me a bit. The chocolate covered corn flakes were obviously a dessert but I wasn't sure about the pears and tuna. Not wanting to cause confusion, I placed them both on the dessert table.

Around the plaza, tables had been set out for everybody to eat and drink at. Inevitably we ended up with Van Cleef and Encarna. Knowing how the Spanish love any affection bestowed upon their children, I turned to the young mother next to me and began stroking the baby's jet-black hair. "*Muy bonito, y tiene mucho pello.*" While still ruffling the baby's hair, I turned my head to Heather and repeated, "I'm just saying, Heather, what a pretty baby and what a lot of hair." Heather looked a little embarrassed and spoke out of the corner of her mouth whilst trying to maintain a smile. "Alan...the woman's breast feeding!" I swiftly but tactfully removed my hand from the baby's head—at least I was hoping without turning around, that it was still the baby's head I was stroking. "I thought it had a boozer's nose," I added.

It was interesting to watch the various dishes being brought to the square. Most of which had silver foil covering them. One man walked past our table with a large tureen, again covered in foil. The reason this one caught my eye was because there was a tail sticking out from underneath the cover and hanging over the edge. "Have you seen Ollie and Digby today?" I asked Heather, who I am sure was thinking the same thing. Noticing my prolonged gaze, Encarna leaned over and said. "*Jabali.*" Wild boar.

A cheer rang out of nowhere when a *paella* in the traditional 4ft pan was produced and a queue immediately formed. While the people tucked in, Paco announced that everybody was free to peruse the food on the tables, but not to touch it yet.

Heather excused herself and went back to our house to the toilet. Encarna passed me a plastic knife and fork. "I'll get something later," I said.

"Allaaan, there is no later!" As I puzzled over this comment, Paco announced his permission to start on the food.

I have never seen anything like it. You would think that these people had not eaten for weeks; they went through the food like a plague of locusts, shovelling anything and everything onto their paper plates until they could hold no more. Others just leaned over the dishes, eating where they stood. That was until they came to our donation. Just as they were going to plunge their forks into the chocolate corn flakes they hesitated, leant forward, sniffed them, stood up straight and prodded them to see if they were alive, then, decision made, shovelled them on to the their plates with what ever else they had managed to forage.

Heather returned, sat down, and then looked around. "What the hell happened here?" Apart from one or two people scraping the bottom of bowls, the centre of the plaza was empty, not only of people but all the food as well. I was explaining what had taken place when Encarna returned to the table, licking her lips and wiping her chin. She shrugged her shoulders and said, "I warned you."

For some reason the only snippet of food left on display was a large cake with just one segment removed. "I wonder what was wrong with that?"

"I don't know," said Heather, "but I bet the woman that made it will be too embarrassed to go and redeem the plate from beneath it."

Heather's sister Pamela popped out for another visit but this time she brought along Gavin. We didn't know much about Gavin, only that he was Pamela's new boyfriend and she had found him on the Internet. Heather refused point blank when I suggested we christen him with the nickname E-Bay. Having Gavin visit was like a breath of fresh air. His laugh and sense of humour were contagious. The only comparison I can imagine is having Peter Kay visit for a week.

The first night I went into the lounge to find a small, unpleasant package presumably left by one of the cats. I walked past Heather in the hallway muttering to myself. "What's wrong?" she asked.

"Those bloody cats," I said guiding Heather back into the lounge. She bent down for a closer look.

"That's not real," She said. At this I bent down for a closer look. Not convinced, I got a bit of tissue and gave it a nudge. Behind me Gavin and Pamela were laughing.

Later in the bar and armed with the aforementioned plastic faeces, I saw young José dashing around acting as tonight's waiter. He would go to the bar with the orders, load up his large tray, come back outside and distribute the drinks and *tapas*. On one of these occasions he stood at the bar as Fernando helped collate the drinks and food. Just as the tray was almost full I dropped the false, plastic 'what's it' into the middle of the tray.

Back at the table we waited and eventually out came José, tray laden with bottles, glasses and *tapas*. At one of the busier tables he began off loading the beverages. All of a sudden he froze, then he raised the tray so the people seated at the table couldn't see the offending object, he smiled and continued asking who ordered this and that. As he finished I tapped him on the shoulder and said, "I think that's mine." When he realised the doggy doo was fake, the expression he had was of not knowing whether to kiss me or kill me.

Gavin then pulled something else from his arsenal of practical jokes; it was circular and made of steal. I looked at it and shrugged my shoulders. Gavin winked then slid away behind Van Cleef's car. I could see him slipping the metal thing into his exhaust.

Thirty minutes later I had almost forgotten what he had done, until Van Cleef bid goodnight, got into his car, and drove away. The whistling/screeching noise could be heard at the other end of the village. As Van Cleef only lives 200 metres from the bar, we left it a couple of minutes then sneaked over to his house to retrieve the insert from his exhaust. As we returned to the bar I shoved it into Manuel's, the builder's, car. I wonder how many people were queued up at the local garage the next day, all with the same complaint.

Later that week we drove over to Balerma to see Carol and Bernie. It was whilst walking through the village that we encountered an elderly Spanish woman carrying 2 large shopping bags, her frail legs buckling under the weight. "Look at that," said Gavin as he went to offer assistance. He approached the woman and gestured that he would carry the bags. She smiled back but shook her head side to side. "Please let me help." Gavin was now becoming insistent. The woman refused once again, only the smile had disappeared. Finally Gavin reached for the bags. The woman muttered something about all the English being insane, turned her back to him and entered the door of the house behind her. Apparently, the reason she was refusing his offer of help was because she had arrived at her destination.

On the last night we all returned to Fernando's bar for what is becoming the traditional send off. The place wasn't particularly busy and the atmosphere was quite subdued. One of the children had just finished playing with a remote controlled car and before going inside the bar he placed the large hand held remote on the table next to ours. "Alan, make your mobile ring," Gavin whispered to me.

"Why?" I asked.

"Just do it," He repeated. So out came my rather dated mobile and within a few seconds it was giving out the incoming call chime. Gavin jumped up causing his chair to slide backwards, which in turn made most of the people outside the bar look up. He walked over to the next table picked up the car remote and pulled the 3ft arial out fully, and then he put the whole thing to the side of his head.

"Hello!" he shouted, "Oh hello mum….. yes we're having a great time, the weather is fantastic." The locals looked at him as though he was mental. "Yes mum, I bought you a thimble from Iznajar… Pam? Yes she's fine." By now Gavin was strolling around the tables. Old Fernando came out carrying a tray, stopped and just stared at him. "Hang on mum." Gavin put his free hand over the face of the remote, turned to old Fernando and said, "It's me mum … *me telefóno muy grande and muy oldy.*" Fernando shook his head and mumbled something similar to the Spanish woman in Balerma, before distributing the drinks on his tray.

"Hang on mum, I'll put her on, Pam me mum wants to speak to you." By now we were creased up, Pam just waved away the offer of the remote control.

"Speak to his mum." Heather said seriously.

"Heather it's not real," I explained, not sure if she hadn't realised or was just entering into the joke.

"No, sorry mum she's busy… anyway I'll have to go….. yes okay, bye." At that Gavin pulled in the arial, replaced the remote on the table next to us, sat down, and picked up his drink. He caught the eye of an old man at the table in front of ours. "Mothers eh… tut." He said. Then he continued his drink as though nothing had happened.

It wasn't only us Brits entering into these jovial japes. Manuel the builder was working on a house and managed to slip a remote fart machine into the pocket of a Welsh man building a small wall across from where Manuel was working. As he stopped to wish the passing Spanish a good day, Manuel would activate the fart machine. The poor man could be seen panicking as he struggled to find the Spanish for, "Sorry but it wasn't me!"

E-MAIL
FROM Stacey/Ashlie/Scott
When I said bungee jumping was the scariest thing I was wrong! SKYDIVING from 12,000 feet is THE scariest thing!

Scott was in the first group to go and Stacey and me were in the next plane, it was tiny. As we climbed high above the cloud (we'd had to wait all day for some gaps so we could jump.) I thought to myself. "If this plane crashes I'm a gonna." Then I remembered I was going to step out of the open door in a few minutes.

When the time came we all, attached to our instructors, shuffled towards the door. As each pair left, the plane rocked from side to side. When it was my turn the instructor said "Just remember to keep your head and legs back." Following his advice I had my head so far back I was almost kissing my arse goodbye. Another instructor was diving at the side of us taking photos and video. When I get back I'll show you it, you've never seen such a nervous, false smile in your life.

Coming home soon, we can't believe it's nearly all over.
Bye
Stacey, Ashlie and Scott x
Ps Going walking on the glaciers tomorrow.

I can't believe it's nearly over and they are all still in one piece.

It wasn't long before our next visitors from the UK turned up. Phil and Yvonne have been friends of ours for nearly 30 years. Phil (a 20 stone prison officer) has been visiting his father's place in Tenerife for the last 20 years, so when I asked if he could speak any Spanish, he replied, "Alan, I'm international me." What he omitted from this sentence was the word incident at the end. Although the British might have found his bottom burps highly amusing, the locals didn't quite get the joke and when Lee Van Cleef asked why he wasn't playing bingo, the reply, "it's for puffs," was thankfully lost in translation. Nevertheless the locals here took both Phil and Yvonne under their wing, as they do everybody, and welcomed them into our tightly knit community.

At the bar one night, Manuel, the chap who'd been in charge of building our pool, invited us all to a bull fight the following night, apparently there was a coach load going.

We met at a bar just outside the village, and as we boarded the coach we were all given a hat and a bandana with one of the matador's names on it. We arrived at a brand new stadium in Granada, our seats only feet from where the action was to take place. I have never been a fan of bull fighting but thought it would be interesting to see, and thought it was only fair to see what it was I was criticising.

The bull charged out and was taunted by a few junior matadors. Then two horses, blindfolded and padded, were ridden out by riders with long spears. As the bull charged the horses the riders stabbed the bull in the back and gave the spear a good twist.

After 5 minutes of this, the horses left the arena and in strode the main man. The matador was about 23 years old, wearing the traditional dress and what could only have been a very large sock stuffed down the front of his trousers. For some reason Heather and Yvonne shuffled in their seats and leant forward. I tried to convince them that this must have been some kind of protective padding but they refused to listen and have their fantasies dashed. When he turned around he revealed one of the tightest arses ever.... even I had to stare....only kidding.... well only for a minute.

Each time the bull got near the matador, or on one occasion even tossed him in the air, Heather, Phil, Yvonne and I cheered the bull. Eventually, due to the disconcerting stares, we felt it diplomatic to watch in silence.

After the bull had been chased about and bled until he was on his last legs, the matador would pull a sword from beneath the cape and plunge it into the bull's spine, killing him instantly—or that was the theory. In reality it actually took the matador half a dozen attempts. In the end you could almost hear the bull saying, "Just bloody do it and get it over with!"

The whole event was judged by some VIP who looked like one of the cast of *The Godfather*. If he thought the kill had been a good one, he would put up his thumb and the bull's ears would be cut off and thrown into the crowd... good wholesome entertainment...unless you are the bull of course.

When the evening was over and we were outside the arena, all the matadors were carried out on the fans' shoulders. They then mingled with the crowd while people had their photograph taken with them. It was here that I actually spotted Yvonne taking a close-up of one of the matador's rear end, unless she was aiming, waiting for him to turn around.

The next day I was talking to one of the young lads in the village, telling him that we had been to a bullfight. Without a word he walked off. Five minutes later he returned waving a leaflet. "Looook Allaaan," he said, "me and you." The leaflet was an advert for anybody who wanted bullfighting lessons. "Mee and you on Saturday, s*i*?"

I pointed out that, unfortunately, I would be busy that day— doing what? I hadn't yet decided. Lee van Cleef had been listening and added in Spanish, "That's not a problem, we will just go into the *campo* (Countryside) and find one to practice on."

"I can' wait!" I said.

The following night we went to a nearby village for a meal. Halfway through the second course, Phil announced he was going to the toilet. As he passed me I thought he might need to know the word for toilet in Spanish in case he had to ask for directions.

"Phil... *Los Servicios*," I said to him quietly.

"No problem Alan, I've already ordered the drinks." You can take the lad out of Leeds but you can't take Leeds out of the lad.

The last day I suggested they might like to visit Granada, so off we went. The idea was to park in the train station and walk into the centre, about half a mile. Then get a bus up the hill that overlooks the Alhambra. I knew that Yvonne was not keen on walking but after a couple of hundred yards she stamped her feet and announced. "Put me in a bar, I'm going no further." After a rest and a cool drink we convinced her to carry on.

Once we stepped off the bus at the top of the hill we looked out on to one of the most incredible views in the world. "Wasn't it worth it?" I asked.

"No," she replied.

I pointed down into the city. "The car is parked just down there. It won't take us 5 minutes to walk back."

"It might not take you that long but I'm getting a taxi." The lack of taxis meant Yvonne had to complete the rest of the journey on foot. Back at the house Yvonne disappeared upstairs and had a 3-hour siesta to recover from the day.

The next day we watched Phil and Yvonne board the plane back to the UK. When we returned home we found a card they had left expressing how much they had enjoyed the holiday and meeting our new friends and how they are looking forward to the next visit.

Chapter 14
The Hunt

I have tried to involve myself as much as possible with village life, but when Van Cleef suggested I accompany him and his son, Raul, on a hunting expedition I must admit I was a little hesitant. "What are we going to be hunting for?" I enquired.

"*Conejo.*" Rabbit, he said. I accepted his invitation and agreed to meet up with them the following Saturday. The night before, Van Cleef came around to our house. "*Allaaan, tenemos un problema.*" We have a problem, he said, and then went on to explain. Apparently in Spain before you can go hunting you have to study and pass an exam first.

"How much studying?" I asked cautiously.

"You can study the book at home and take the exam in Granada," he explained.

"How thick is this book and is it in Spanish?"

"Of course its in Spanish, it's about 400 pages," he said in a matter-of-fact-way.

"I think I'll pass if you don't mind." It would appear my Elmer Fudd days have been cut short.... Pesky wabbits.

"Okay you can come with us but you can't shoot," was the compromise he came up with.

The next day I was up at 6am. We drove into the *campo*, accompanied by Raul, and spent the next four hours trudging around following a pack of dogs that looked like they hadn't been fed for weeks.

It was remarkable the amount of rabbit holes that we saw, yet no rabbits. Had Andalucia suffered the previous year from the scourge of myxomatosis, and nobody had told these two?

Bang! Van Cleef's gun going off scared me half to death. We searched the vicinity but found nothing. "*¿No lo has visto?*" he asked dejectedly.

"No. I didn't see anything."

Ten minutes later another bang just a few feet away scared the lot of us. Another hunter emerged from behind a large tree, gun still smoking. He jumped with alarm when he saw us. As everybody was wearing camouflaged jackets, I was beginning to doubt how safe any of us were out here. I wish I'd have brought a fluorescent jacket.

Van Cleef greeted the newcomer, who informed us that he was just one of four sweeping through the woods in a line. It was decided we would tag along on the end and continue along with them. With so many guns around I walked behind Van Cleef, believing it to be the safest option. That was until he threw his gun on to his shoulder so it was facing me. Now, if I'd wanted to spend my afternoons looking down the twin barrels of a shotgun I would have bought a post office in Manchester. I tactfully moved slightly to the right, out of direct fire, and walked on like the obedient dogs.

Bang! One of the other men had fired and we all stopped. The rabbit had eluded the hunter further up the line and now ran across the field in front of us. Within seconds Van Cleef had positioned the gun into his shoulder, aimed and fired. Bang!

We strolled over to find the rabbit lying with its eyes still open but definitely dead. Van Cleef picked it up, winked, and then fed its back legs through a loop on his belt. I noticed his breathing had become more rapid. As we continued I couldn't take my eyes off the small body, I even found myself humming 'Bright Eyes.'

Looking up I could see dozens of pigeons flying above us. I tapped my escort on the shoulder, pointed sky wards and whispered. "*¿Más facil, no?*" The birds did look an easier option.

"*No es possible, otra vez sera,*" said Van Cleef. Presumably out of season and boy did they know it. They swooped and dived right above us, I'm sure they were aiming at us, trying to do their business right above our heads. Now I knew how the rabbits felt.

The rabbit on the belt kept catching on the thorn bushes we moved through, so eventually it was taken off the belt and shoved into a large pocket, especially designed for the job, in the back of his hunting jacket.

Ten minutes later and Bang! Another rabbit had dared to cross our path. On this occasion Van Cleef had missed, but loading another two cartridges, he wasn't going to let it get away. Bang! I saw the creature jump as it made for the safety of a small bush. Van Cleef bent down for a better shot. Bang! Knowing he'd got it he smiled over his shoulder, once again his breathing shallow and rapid.

I let him retrieve the prey and as he returned I noticed it twitching. "*¿Muerte?*" Dead? I asked. He held it up by its back legs and once again the head moved. Van Cleef gave the back of its head a sharp crack with the side of his hand. "*Sí,*" he said shoving this one into the same large pocket as the other.

We continued walking. I couldn't help noticing the stain on the outside of his 'special' pocket increasing in size. As the day wore on the heat increased, and so did the flies, probably attracted by the smell. It is difficult to describe the smell; of course it could simply be Van Cleef, who was sweating profusely, as were we all. I won't be melodramatic and describe it as the stench of death, because never having smelt it I wouldn't know, but it's how I imagine it.

I mentioned as we walked that I was a little thirsty. Raul snatched a pomegranate growing wild on a nearby bush. He crushed it with all the force he could muster, removed his knife from the sheaf on his belt and made a small hole. Hey presto, an instant drink.

After 5 hours walking up and down through the most inhospitable of terrain, I had to admit that I was completely exhausted. We turned the corner and there was Van Cleef's car. "Thank God for that," I said to myself, but retracted it immediately as we walked straight past it.

We must have walked in another circle because 30 minutes later I could see the car again. Another pigeon flew above us. Van

Cleef tilted his shotgun upwards and pulled the trigger. Bang! The bird dropped like a stone. I frowned. Had I misunderstood the previous explanation why we weren't hunting pigeons? No, as Van Cleef smiled out the side of his mouth he placed his forefinger to his lips and said, "Ssshhhh." He then made the sign as if he were zipping his mouth closed. Picking the bird up he looked around to see if anybody was looking, then rammed it into the 'special' pocket, this time he zipped it shut.

"¿Qué haces?" What are you doing? asked one of our shooting companions, emerging from some bushes. Fortunately he was one of Van Cleef's best friends. I had to smile as Van Cleef spun around trying to wipe the feathers from his hands, and with the expression of a naughty schoolboy answered, *"¡Nada!"* (Nothing!)

Although I believed I'd been brought along as an extra set of eyes, I had decided from now on to keep any observations with regards the wild life to myself. How many did he need? Van Cleef had explained that he normally shoots 7 or 8 in one trip, so as we drove home I felt as though he blamed me in some way for today's poor showing.

He dropped me back at the house tired and hungry and thirsty. "How did it go?" Heather asked. I withheld most of the details, as I know Heather isn't keen on that sort of thing. "Oh fine, educational," I added.

Changing the subject I decided to show her the trick Raul had done with the pomegranate. I removed one from the fruit bowl and began squeezing it as hard as I could. I think it's safe to say that Heather was less than impressed. At least we now know what the kitchen would look like if we decided to paint everything red... Ever seen a pomegranate explode?

Two weeks later I was once again invited to hunt. Caught off guard, I couldn't think of an excuse quick enough why not to go, but I am assured tomorrow will be different. We are going for, I can't remember the name of the bird, but Van Cleef reminded me that we had once had it for Sunday dinner at his house...So that's what it was.

"We will have to sit and wait in silence and keep looking all the time," He warned. I thought this an ideal time to wind him up. "Can I take a radio?" I asked. He slapped the palm of his hand against his forehead and repeated, *"Silencio."*

After a brief conversation with Paco, the game warden, not the domino player, (If you want to picture him, by the way, he is the double of 'Norm' from the 80s comedy *Cheers*.) it was agreed that I would be okay to actually use a gun. I didn't quite catch all of Van Cleef's pitch on my behalf, I heard 'military' and 'trained' I'm sure, and I also heard Afghanistan and Vietnam. I was a little worried he was slightly exaggerating. I had in fact only served six years in the RAF reserves. A simple nod of Paco's head was all that was needed. When it came I bet the message went out throughout the aviary world to run or fly for the hills...NOT!

I was picked up at 3pm on Saturday and off we went into the *campo* (countryside). After driving through all kinds of terrain we saw about 10 birds sitting in a field. Van Cleef pointed these out and explained that these are what we will be hunting. Another 50 yards away, a few more ran across the road in front of the car, and we nearly ran them over. "This is going to be easy," I thought. "There's hundreds of them."

Eventually we parked the car under a tree and began to unload. I got to carry a big cream cushion, a cage with a cover over it, and an axe. Van Cleef carried the guns, a camouflage screen, a folding stool, and a stand for the birdcage. In the words of *Alice in Wonderland*...."It gets curiouser and curiouser."

Now at this time I think it's better explained if I put everything into a time frame....you'll see.

3:37pm

We set the birdcage up on its stand and removed the cover. Van Cleef said, "When it sings other birds will come". We then retired about 30 yards to a group of bushes. I was surprised to see 4 shotgun cartridges, 2 empty, cigarette packets, and about 30-tab end on the ground. This was obviously his tried and tested spot. He used his axe to cut away some bush that blocked our vision and set up the screen. The cream cushion was for me...thank God.

3:55pm

We were all set up, guns loaded and both watching proceedings through our respective peepholes. I was quite impressed with how well hidden we were, that was until the master lit up his first cigarette. We could be seen for miles, but he was the expert.

4:32pm

Nothing, absolutely sod all. Van Cleef looked at me and whispered, "She doesn't want to sing."

I whispered back, "She's probably waiting for music. I told you I should have brought a radio." I had to put my hand over my mouth to stop myself from laughing. Even he gave a smirk.

4:45pm

All was not lost. We moved to plan 'B'. Van Cleef had brought a reserve for just such a situation. So off he went to take the original bird back to the car and bring out another. At last the opportunity came to stand up and stretch my legs.

4:58pm

Back in our positions of stealth we waited once again. Before we had set off I had anticipated we might be sitting in an uncomfortable position for a long time, and my bad back being the cross I bear nowadays I pre-empted any problems by taking a 'special' before we set off. No, I'm not a crazed druggy. A 'special' is what we call the tablets I take when suffering like only a man knows. The fact that they are codeine based means that when they 'kick in', any pain anywhere vanishes. Unfortunately there are a number of side effects:

1. You become very relaxed and sigh a lot.

2. You start to tell people you love them... one I held back, as whispering to Van Cleef in our current situation may be perceived by some as a little inappropriate. Especially bearing in mind he is holding a loaded shotgun.

3. This one I had no control over. When you take these tablets on an empty stomach, the insides of the aforementioned stomach announces the fact to all within ear shot.... It rumbles for England.

5:05pm

Van Cleef looks at me as if I am making my stomach growl on purpose. I, in return whisper, "Wouldn't it be easier going to the supermarket?"

"No, you can't buy these at the supermarket," he grunted back

5:08pm

Most of the birds we have heard seemed to be calling from behind us. All of a sudden there is a weird noise. The bird singing sounds like a cross between R2D2 from *Star Wars* and Dick Dastardly's side kick from *'Catch the Pigeon'*, the one with tourettes. If you can't remember him just think of Pete, the winner of *Big Brother* 2006…on speed.

This bird carries on with this annoying song for the rest of the time we are here.

5:15pm

At this precise moment a duck billed platypus, including elongated beak, appears right over our heads. I considered pointing this out to my partner in crime but didn't think he would share my appreciation for unusual cloud formations, and he would have torn a strip off me for not watching our decoy, who not only refused to sing like its predecessor, but I think had gone to sleep.

5:31pm

In the bar the previous night I had asked how long we would be hunting. The reply was from 3pm until about 6pm………. OH MY GOD! I've got a cramp!

I tried to stretch out my leg but as our shelter was full of broken twigs and dead leaves, the slightest noise seemed magnified. Another disapproving glance from my comrade in arms.

5:38pm

Van Cleef has looked at his watch at least 4 times in the last 2 minutes. It was like a football referee advertising the end of the game is imminent. Hang on. A different kind of birdcall woke our decoy. She spread her wings and called back. I'm not sure what she said but the bird doing the original calling immediately flew off ….. I wonder if birds have a time of the month.

5:56pm

We throw in the towel and admit defeat. This is the second time we have been hunting and returned with less than expected. If this goes on I will be known in the village as, *El Jonah* of Spanish hunting.

6:03pm

Car loaded up, we set off back to the village. On more than one occasion we pass a group, or gaggle, or whatever a group of our elusive prey are called. Now I'm not sure birds can either point or laugh but—I don't know, it must have been my imagination.

Did you know how R2D2 from *Star Wars* got his name? When filming, they hadn't agreed on the name for the robot. Then somebody saw R2D2 on a can of film, it meant 'Reel 2 Day 2'. Well that's what I heard anyway.

So we returned to the village empty handed. It's funny how every time Van Cleef goes hunting without me he returns with numerous tales of successful kills. I wonder if he goes fishing as well.

Chapter 15
It's the Police!

Another Saturday and another day out. Where? I haven't the foggiest idea. Once again, during the week, Van Cleef had said in passing that he would be picking us up at about 10am on Saturday morning. "To go where?" I asked.

"*Es la Dia de la Guardia.*" *Guardia* or *Guardia Civil*, as the police are called, apparently have their own special day. "What happens?" I asked.

The reply, "You will see," was what I was expecting.

"*¿Qué ropas?*" What clothes do I need to wear? I asked. As far as I knew we could be doing anything from paintballing to ballet.

"*El traje, porqué primero vamos al iglesia.*" So I needed a suit as it started at a church, and that's more than I usually find out on these expeditions.

Saturday came and Heather and I looked like we were dressed for a wedding. Van Cleef pulled up outside the house and beeped his horn. He entered the house dressed as I was in a suit and asked me the question he always does on these occasions, which was to fasten his tie. For some reason he could never do it properly. Encarna was dressed in a typical Spanish dress complete with hair done and makeup, something you don't see often.

We drove around the corner and stopped outside the village shop. When I asked why we'd stopped, Encarna who was getting out of the car at the time, lifted her dress and showed us the ladder in her tights. It seemed to end beyond where a lady would be prepared to show.

Down in Loja, outside the large church, we struggled to find a parking place. Whilst everybody else jockeyed for position, Van Cleef simply pulled up onto the curb and abandoned his vehicle. We all got out of the car, apart from Encarna who was shuffling around in the back, legs in the air, trying to replace her tights. Walking down to the church I feel she lost a little bit of that air of mystique that I feel the Latin women have when wearing full regalia. Watching her walk with one hand up the front of her dress and the other tugging from the rear, didn't really convey the same look that the post cards often display.

Whenever we go to the bar on a Friday there are always at least half a dozen members of the *Guardia Civil* there. So I wasn't surprised to see them here today. What I didn't realise is the men that go in the bar are the top brass of Loja's finest.

There they stood outside the church greeting people as they arrived, each one wearing more gold braid than a Japanese general. "*Hola Allaaan y Heder.*" Like everybody else, they never could pronounce Heather. We all shook hands and entered the church. The place was cram packed with men in uniform and their families. All four of us managed to squeeze onto a pew at the back and the service began.

After about fifteen minutes a couple of woman in there 20s came in a side door and stood at the back near us. Van Cleef stood up and offered his seat to one of them. I of course had to do likewise but hesitated due to the fact that I had injured my back, again, the previous day and had an idea this wasn't going to be a short service.

An hour and twenty minutes later the service drew to a close. Heather, recognising my hesitation to give up my seat, joined me and asked, "How's your back?" On reflection, my reply of "Better if those fat birds had arrived on time!" was a little un-gentlemanly.

We all piled back into the car, both Heather and I assuming we were going back to the village. Instead, we drove to the other side of town to one of the big hotels. The inside of the main hall had been set out in the style of an expensive wedding reception. This was for the special guests of the day. A television cameraman filmed everybody entering. I later found out that we had appeared on Loja T.V.

As the bar was crowded, one of the top brass came over to our little group, along with his wife, and suggested we might get served quicker in the public restaurant attached to the hotel. You should have seen the faces of the people in the restaurant as the police officer, looking like a Japanese general, followed by me and Van Cleef, wearing black suits, along with our partners and a film crew, all strolled through to the bar. I've never been pointed and talked about so much in my life, it was great.

Back where we were supposed to be, the meal was coming to an end and the top table had progressed on to the speeches. I noticed we were the only English present and nobody was doing any translating for us, so we just sat there watching.

"*Antonio Lucena, por favor*," called one of the speechmakers. Recognising the name of one of the men that come to the bar, I asked Van Cleef what was happening. Through the cheers I managed to grasp that he was retiring and moving away.

I later found out why Antonio Lucena had shed the odd tear whilst accepting his parting gift. The *Guardia* are almost like the military wing of the police and as such live in barracks. Antonio had been a member of the *Guardia* all his life and now at the age of 55 he was leaving all his comrades, the job he had loved for nearly 40 years, and, as he was leaving the area, most of his friends as well.

As the celebrations at the hotel wound down, a nod of Van Cleef's head in the direction of the door told me it was time to go. It was 10:30pm and we had been at it all day. Halfway along the road home, Encarna, our designated driver, indicated right and turned. "Where are we going? asked Heather. A large sign in front of us read. GUARDIA CIVIL – LOJA. "I don't think the party is over yet," I answered. The garage that housed all the police cars and the police motorbikes had been cleared out and decorated with bunting, balloons, and a bar—a 'free' bar at that. "How long does this go on till?" I asked Van Cleef.

He held up three fingers. "*Tres días.*"

I turned to Heather. "I hope there's a break in between," I said as I accepted the drinks being passed over from the bar.

During the evening we were introduced to Paco (no not the domino player or the compere) and his wife Laura. Because our Spanish is not very good they tried to speak English, which wasn't particularly very good either. So we ended up with the bizarre situation where we were speaking Spanish and they were speaking English. I asked where they work, and eventually understood that they worked in some kind of records office in Loja. Laura explained further that they keep all the records on deeds, house purchases, planning permissions, etc.

I didn't mention the pool.

I did mention that our house was a new one and voiced my concern that as a foreigner you never know if everything had been carried out as it should have been. Paco asked for our details, which I handed over a little nervously. Three days later he phoned to say that he had checked and everything is perfect with regards to the paperwork for our house. Phew!

E-MAIL
FROM Stacey/Ashlie/Scott
Hey all, hope everyone is fine and dandy.

Well who can say they have lived with 30 Koreans...Us! We are back in Sydney with only 2 more days left in Australia. We are in a hostel run by Koreans and are the only white people around (Scott has been trying to explain the difference, looking wise, between Thai, Chinese and Korean people, but I can't yet see it!).

We are in an 8-bed dorm and the view from the kitchen is of a sex shop across the road with all the outfits clearly on display in the window. Oh I forgot to mention the line of prostitutes waiting to be picked up! Yes you guessed it we are in Kings Cross just outside the centre of Sydney (also known as the red light district). Our roommates are all friendly, although they find it difficult to understand our accent so we have to speak really slowly! Australians can't even understand our accent so God help people who are still learning English!

Last night we went to a bar that was having a quiz competition. A novelty question came up and the first person to shout out got a free jug of beer. "What stays in the house..." the girl started to say and Scott stood up and shouted out "the wife!" Well that got all the females booing and the blokes cheering. Needless to say we didn't get the prize.

Got to go now, see you soon in the flesh.

Stacey Ashlie and Scott x

They also mentioned in a phone call that they would be staying in Leeds for a couple of weeks before flying out to Spain. "Heather," I said whilst doing a quick calculation on my fingers, "that means they will be here at the same time as your parents." We checked the calendar, and yes they would overlap, but only for a day.

The car had been playing up and as the nearest SAAB dealer was over 40 miles away it was becoming a real problem. I had also been weighing up the advice we had received about keeping our English car over here, without going through the proper procedure of having it reregistered and putting on Spanish plates. It had crossed my mind on more than one occasion how the authorities would look upon it if we were to have a serious crash. Aside from the authorities, if a large payout was needed then I am sure the insurance company would look deeper into any claim for a way out of paying.

We had discovered a way to get the road tax paid; a new system meant that you could do it on-line. Now I know that most of the English that still use their English plated cars don't bother with any kind of MOT, and those that do put their cars in and have the Spanish equivalent, the ITV. To be honest I am not entirely convinced that the ITV is recognised by the British Department of Transport, therefore the car is probably being driven illegally and any insurance they do have would be void.

Not wanting to have to deal with such a problem we agreed to change the car. We would buy a new Spanish plated one and drive the SAAB back to the UK when we went to meet our intrepid travellers, the girls and Scott.

So all we had to do now was pick one. How hard can it be? We visited most of the car dealers in Granada and eventually chose a Citroen C4 (the one that turns into a robot on the T.V. ad). With a previous quote in hand we returned to make our purchase, Javier came along as the salesman we had spoken to didn't speak any

English, and when you're spending €15,000 you don't want any mistakes.

The first thing we did was to sit at the other side of the salesman's desk and listen to Javier start speaking. A small argument ensued resulting in the salesman walking off. *"¿Hay un problema?"* Is there a problem? I asked Javier. He replied with a smile and a wink.

Five minutes later the salesman returned and presented us with a revised quote, €300 less than the previous one. Javier later informed me that he had told the salesman that we had been offered the same car for €300 less at another garage. Reluctantly the salesman had agreed to match it. With a few minor hiccups the paperwork was completed and we were told we would get a phone call in a week or so, confirming the car was ready to be picked up.

Four days later I get a call. I have always, for some reason, found it harder to understand Spanish over the phone. All I grasped was that there had been a problem registering the car and I had to visit the '*Hacienda*'. Unfortunately, the only *Hacienda* I knew of had been on the hit western *Bonanza*, or was it *High Chaparral*? As I put the phone down the doorbell rang, it was Encarna, Van Cleef's wife, with Heather's Avon. (See, it's not that much different over here.) I asked if she would ring the garage and speak to the salesman to find out what the problem was. "*Sí, no problema*," she said as I passed her the number.

After a swift conversation, she hung up, turned to face me, and said in Spanish, "You need to go to the *Hacienda*"..... Back to square one.

"*Sí, pero ¿qué es la Hacieda y dónde?*" What is it and where is it? I asked. She then offered her and Van Cleef's services as escorts the following morning.

We pulled up outside a large white building next to the police station in the centre of Loja. As we entered, we passed through a metal detector. I still had no idea where we were or why we had to be there. Van Cleef walked up to a uniformed man and spent the next 5 minutes pointing to me and coming out with as many obscenities and expletives as he could think of. I understood the words: idiot, dick head, fool and the inevitable… English!

After filling in a form and passing it back to a clerk he printed off another form and gave it to Van Cleef, who in turn passed it to me. When I looked at it all I could see was a sheet of labels with bar codes printed on them. "You can be getting your nooo car now," said the clerk with a wave.

To this day I have no idea what that was all about.

Chapter 16
Together Again

We had decided to surprise Stacey, Ashlie, and Scott at Manchester airport. We drove back to the UK in the SAAB with the intention of leaving it with Allan, a friend, to sell on our behalf.

We stayed at Phil and Yvonne's house, as they were on holiday, and were quite impressed with the security measures around the house. All doors locked and bolted including internal ones, there were grills on the back door, alarms, and the neighbourhood watch officials constantly patrolling. Being a prison officer I assumed it was all just habit.

I did think the cosh under the bed was slightly worrying, and the hammer in the magazine rack was unnerving. When they returned from holiday I queried this with Phil. He then showed me the 'wanted' posters the prisoners had made. I couldn't help but smile when he was referred to as 'The fat salad dodger'. I suggested to Heather that if during the night it became suddenly warm then it wouldn't be me going through the change, and pointed out that there was no electric blanket, so it would probably be a fire bomb.

We managed to surprise our fearless travellers at the airport, as they thought that it was only Heather's father, Brian, picking them up. Whilst waiting for them at arrivals we discussed to what extent they would have changed. Would they look different? Have an Oz accent? Become more mature? Within an hour all our questions were answered… Ashlie still talks for England, Stacey is still as dizzy as ever, and Scott's jokes still weren't funny.

Whilst back in the UK we decided to take the opportunity to try and catch up with everybody. Most of the time during the day was spent at my parent's house. My father had deteriorated quite a bit and didn't get out of his chair much. Next to him was an array of medication, inhalers, tablets, bottles of medicine, and even a Nebulizer. His speech was worse than the day I had left him in the hospital, and his memory, or lack of it, infuriated him. The weight had fallen off him, but one thing remained, his sense of humour.

He was now visiting the hospital on almost a weekly basis; often taken by ambulance after another minor stroke or if he had just passed out. The strain was also telling on my mother; she too had lost weight and was beginning to look her age. Although she is 73 years old, most people would guess her to be at least 15 years younger.

On an evening we would visit the houses of friends, family, and neighbours. On one occasion whilst visiting our old neighbours, Brian and Patsy, they had let it slip that Martin and Toni, other neighbours, were expecting…well Toni was. Unfortunately they weren't supposed to have let the cat out of the bag. That meant we had to look surprised when we met up with them that night at a Chinese restaurant.

When we arrived they were all waiting for us. I was dying to walk up to them all and ask, "Just a minute, can I smell fertilized eggs?" but Heather wouldn't let me. Nevertheless, within half an hour I also had let slip that we knew. I am absolutely the last person you want to guard a secret.

The week went very fast and before we knew it we were saying our goodbyes. The girls would be out to join us shortly but saying goodbye to friends and family is never easy. When it came to saying goodbye to my dad he lifted himself from the chair and squeezed me with as much strength as he could muster, which wasn't much. I dared not return the gesture in case I harmed him, he felt so frail.

We returned to Phil and Yvonne's house to commence our packing for the airport. The new restrictions meant that we could only take 20kg each, so for the next hour we switched things and weighed them again, removed more clothes from the cases and weighed yet again. Eventually we realized that the cases themselves weighed 5kg, so on Stacey's advice we put the contents of one of the cases in a large rucksack

Our flight was to leave Liverpool at 5:30am on Thursday. Brian, Heather's father, offered to take us to the airport, but we didn't want him driving us in the early hours, so we agreed to leave at 11pm and just kill time in the airport. Having 6 hours to waste, I tried to sleep, only to be woken up with Heather panicking. Apparently she had reread the flight details and our limit was in fact only 15kg.

For the next hour we opened all our bags and cases, making a pile of non-essentials. I found it hard to believe that Heather thought my Pek Chopped Pork was not an essential, but alas I handed it over.

By the time we had finished, Heather was wearing 2 jumpers, a cardigan, and 2 jackets, whereas I looked like Joey from *Friends*, wearing all Chandler's clothes. All our pockets were filled with socks and underwear. Heather binned the pile of non-essentials and we agreed we would have to pay any excess for what was still over.

I decided to go for a walk as by now, although I looked like I weighed 25 stone and passers by were shouting "fat salad dodger," I was in fact losing 10lb a minute because of sweating so much. I then realised a passenger was already queuing at the 'Granada' check-in desk. I asked her. "What is the baggage restriction?"

"20kg," she replied. Behind me the Ryanair desk had just opened, so I asked them the same question and got the same reply.

"Heather, go and get my bloody Pek Chopped Pork out of that bloody bin," I said, stripping away as many layers as I could.

We arrived back home in Spain and everything was just as we had left it, including the patio door left open so the cats could come and go. Phil and his neighbourhood watch would have had a dickyfit. The cats hadn't missed us and had put on about 4lbs each; Javier had been coming every day to feed them—more fat salad dodgers.

Having been back only a week, we had to dash around cleaning the house in preparation for the visit of Heather's parents, Shirley and Brian. Although they are quite well travelled it will have been the first time they had left the tourists routes and mixed with true locals.

Over the last nearly 30 years Shirley and I have got on like a house on fire, but I can never resist the urge to wind her up. When Heather and I first started seeing each other, Heather used to comment that she didn't know how I got away with some of the things I said and did. "She would have killed any of us for that," Heather would say, referring to herself and her sisters.

The day arrived and after picking them up from the airport we went straight back to the house so they could have a rest. The flight, like ours, had departed from Liverpool airport at about 5:30am so they hadn't managed to get any sleep the previous night.

By lunchtime they both arose from their beds and came downstairs looking totally refreshed. "Fancy a tour around the village?" I asked. The stroll Heather and I often take leads down through the main part of the village and back on to the narrow main road from Loja, eventually ending up back in the village outside Fernando's bar.

Halfway around, we began the gradual climb back toward the village. The road there was, as I said, quite narrow and without footpaths. We continued in single file and, being at the front, I was the first to hear the lorry coming in the opposite direction.

"Keep in, lorry coming!" I shouted, stepping back slightly and waiting for it to pass. As it did, the driver gave a nod of the head and moved into the middle of the road to avoid us. Before I set off again I glanced over my shoulder at the others. Shirley was in the drainage ditch that ran along the side of the road, being helped out by Brian. I knew I shouldn't laugh so I turned away, shoved my fist in my mouth and bit down hard. "I jumped in on purpose," claimed Shirley, as she dusted herself off. Heather gave me a painful jab in the ribs with her elbow.

That night we went into the bar to introduce them to the locals. What Shirley didn't realise was that I knew she would be a little uncomfortable with the Spanish greeting of a kiss on either cheek. So what did I do? I had told Van Cleef, Encarna, and all our friends that she loved it and they had to do it to her every time they saw her. It was great to watch, although I thought Encarna was going a little over the top when Shirley returned from the toilet and she jumped up and pecked her on either cheek.

143

At bingo the following night we sat with the usual crowd and as usual won nothing. I mentioned to Shirley that if she wins she has to shout as loud as she can.

"¡Estoy borracha!" I told her it was Spanish for 'house' and she even got a pen out and wrote the word down so she wouldn't forget it. Unfortunately, she never won, and it's a shame because it actually means "I'm pissed."

Throughout the evening Van Cleef was his usual charming self, no, I'm not being sarcastic. Whenever we have any visitors, he runs around them like a bee arsed fly, getting their drinks and hanging their jacket up; there is no end to his manners. It appears that it's only when I'm with him on his own that he changes into a rough red neck who boasts about how many animals he's slaughtered that day.

As the night wore on, the sound of the television in the background caught my attention. I nodded to Lee Van Cleef and pointed to the TV. It was about 1:30 in the morning and the football highlights had finished, and the programme being shown was a full on porn movie.

When Fernando noticed, he picked up the remote and turned the television to a different channel. Van Cleef shouted an obscenity, went up to the TV, and turned it back to the porn channel. Brian made a few of the locals smile when he jokingly removed his specs and give them a good clean before continuing to watch the television. The funny thing was that only the women seemed to win bingo after that... I wonder why?

Returning home at the end of the night, I climbed the wide stairs that lead to the front door. Admittedly it was quite dark so that was probably why Shirley missed the first step and went arse over tit. As she laid spread eagled I knew she was more embarrassed than hurt but nevertheless could feel my lips going up at each side. Why is it that some people find others' misfortune amusing?

Once again I rammed my fist into my gob and bit down hard. The marks on my knuckles were still visible the next day. By the time Shirley goes home I'm going to look like some sort of self-harmer.

We got her up and into the house and she was fine. The rest of the week was relatively uneventful and Shirley sustained no more injuries. When we went back to the bar later in the week, nobody gave Shirley any additional welcome kisses. When she mentioned this I explained that it had probably been just the novelty of the first night.

Noticing David (pronounced like the Welsh say it, Dav-id) leaving the bar, I called over to him, *"¿Dónde estuviste?"* I asked where he was yesterday because he was supposed to be keeping an appointment his mother made for him. I was to give him an English lesson. He simply shrugged his shoulders and left. Later I saw one of his friends and mentioned his misdemeanour. "I'm going to give him a hundred lines," I said jokingly.

"You should make him do what we had to do at primary school."

"What was that? I asked.

"You had to go to the corner of the classroom and kneel on dry peas for ages."

I pondered this for a while and asked, "Did you go to the primary school in the local village, or were you educated at a detention centre in Baghdad?"

Heather and I had lived without the girls for almost a year, and without realising it we had gotten into a routine. All that was about to change.

Chapter 17
An English Fiesta

Stacey, Ashlie, and Scott arrived at the airport in Granada not really knowing what to expect from Spain, and not knowing what they were going to do with the rest of their lives. A year is a long time in a short life and although I joked earlier about how they may have changed, it wasn't to be long before it was confirmed that neither of them had changed one iota.

Stacey and Ashlie had always been walking disasters. I'm sure they possessed some kind of kinetic energy that would make things shatter, break, or simply stop working whenever they got within ten feet of anything. The first night, just before we went to bed, Stacey knocked a large glass bottle onto the kitchen floor. It smashed into the smallest pieces you have ever seen. Over the last year whilst apart from the kids, I had acquired an inner calm, an almost tranquil state. I smiled, explained it wasn't a problem, and helped her clean up the mess. The following day, Ashlie kicked the pot cat dish and smashed that. "Not to worry," I said and swallowed a deep breath.

I thought it would be a good idea to spend some quality time with the girls so I suggested to Stacey that we should go for a bike ride. Heather and I had only had the bikes a couple of weeks and had only used them once. Fifteen minutes later in the middle of the *campo*, Stacey broke the bike; the pedal came off and wouldn't go back on. You should have seen her trying to peddle back with only one.

I'm sure I'm starting to get a nervous twitch....

We all trailed the 40 miles or so back to the shop we bought the bikes from, as they had been repairing Heather's bike. We collected it and drove home. As we pulled up, Stacey asked, "Can we go out on the bikes now dad?" Why not? I thought.

Ten minutes later Stacey had broken the other pedal. I took the bike back to the shop and told them in no uncertain terms that I wanted my money back. I think we actually spent more on petrol than the bike had costed.

In the bar at the beginning of the week there was a small commotion. Somebody ran through the door shouted something in Spanish too quickly for me to understand and ran out again. He was followed by half a dozen of the locals. We all looked at each other and wondered if a fight had broken out or something. A departing local stopped at the door turned his head and shouted. *"¡Es verdad!"* It's true! The rest of the bars occupants ran out as well. Not wanting to miss the excitement, we followed them. What was it? It had started to rain. Well, I suppose it was the first time in about 4 months and the olive trees that supplied the livelihood for most of them certainly needed the water.

There is a bitter dispute going on in the household at the moment. You see, Van Cleef's dog just had 4 puppies and he is convinced we are going to have one. In fact, Heather is the only one convinced that we are not. As it stands at the moment we have discovered that our home is not actually a democracy and although the current vote is 3 against 2, the 2's have it, but we'll see.

Every time Heather comes up with a reason not to have a dog, Van Cleef comes straight back at her. For example:

Heather: "We don't have anywhere to keep it."

Van Cleef: "I will build a kennel for it."

Heather: "We can't afford the vet's bills"

Van Cleef: "It's only €20 (£14) to have all its injections and a chip."

Heather: "Where will we put it when we visit the UK?"

Van Cleef. "My house."

Etc, etc, etc. In the end, he nodded to me and whispered. "Allaaan, I will ring your door bell and leave it outside for you." I'm not sure if he was joking or not.

Back in the UK, Allan, the friend who we left the SAAB with to sell on our behalf, rang with a combination of good news and bad. The good news was he sold the car to somebody who left a deposit whilst he carried out a HP check. The bad news is, the HP check came back and the car was shown to be stolen.

You may remember that just before we came out to Spain we were burgled and the car was stolen. Well, according to somebody's records it still was. I rang the DVLA and the police to no avail. So I rang the insurance company we were using at the time it was stolen. After holding on the phone for 40 minutes I explained the problem to the person on the other end. "Ah, you need to speak to our 'stolen car' department. I'll give you their number."

I rang this number and after another 40 minutes I once again explained my dilemma. "So you got the car back?" asked the woman on the other end.

"Yes that's why a year later I'm in the process of selling it," I replied.

"So you don't want to carry on the claim you started making a year ago?"

"No. I explained to someone a year ago that I got it back." I tried to keep my calm.

"So why are you ringing now?" she asked.

"Because apparently you have put it on a list somewhere, and when anybody does a HP check on it, it comes up as stolen." I took a deep breath.

"And what do you want me to do?" she said vaguely.

"Get it off the list so it doesn't show 'stolen' anymore." If I'd been within reach of this woman she would have needed health insurance. In the background I could hear her tapping away at a keyboard. I was half expecting her to say. "The computer says nooooo."

"Done!" she said. So the car sale could go ahead and that was one less thing to worry about.

Over the summer we had attended numerous Spanish fiestas, celebrating this and that. During a discussion about fiestas in general, one of the Spanish lads asked what kind of fiestas we have in the UK. I pondered the question for a minute or two and explained that we don't celebrate all the saints as they do in Spain; we tend to celebrate things like Easter, birthdays, anniversaries, and Christmas, and therefore don't have as many as they do. Plus there is the fact that we don't get the weather to have the big outdoor celebrations that take place in Spain.

Heather reminded me that the following Saturday was to be November the 5th. I turned to the young man and added. "There is one other celebration we have, 'Bonfire Night'."

"¿Qué haces?" What do you do? He asked. With my limited Spanish, I felt going into an explanation about Guy Fawkes was going to be too difficult, so I simply explained what actually takes place. "The children make a dummy of a man with old clothes and during the week before Bonfire night they sit on street corners asking for money."

"Begging?" somebody at the table asked.

"Well sort of," I answered. "Then the night before, on the 4th of November, they go around the streets being mischievous."

"Causing trouble?" asked the same man at the table.

"Well, yes sort of," I said, knowing this was rapidly going downhill.

"What do they do with the money they are begging?" asked a different man.

I thought for a while. "They buy…" I didn't know the Spanish word for fireworks so selected the nearest that I did know, "…explosives." As the conversation continued we attracted more listeners. "On the actual night everybody helps to build large fires. We place the dummy on top, light the fire, and watch him burn." Thinking about it, it all seemed quite macabre. "Once the fire is going we set light to the explosives," I could see they all thought we were completely mad.

"I'll tell you what," I said. "On the 5th we will have a Bonfire outside my house at night time," I suggested.

Van Cleef announced, "Why not have a barbecue in the afternoon?" I could tell this was going to be like no other Bonfire night I'd ever been to.

149

That night we had all agreed to have an early night, and Heather and I stayed up a little longer to give everybody else time to use the bathroom and get ready first.

Outside, a storm that had been brewing all day was just beginning to unleash the torrential rain and cracking thunder that can only be found in the Mediterranean. Or Hull.

Crack!

The thunder sounded like it was just above our heads. That's when I remembered the surprise I had for Stacey. A week earlier Javier had been visiting when, without a word, he stepped outside. We just presumed he had gone for a smoke. All of a sudden there was this terrific bang. We dashed outside to find him with a mischievous grin on his little Spanish chops. "What the hell was that?" I asked. He then went on to show me a small brown paper pouch, about the size of a 50p piece, with a small fuse sticking out. "My friend makes them," he said. I can only assume that his friend works at the quarry or spends his time dismantling shot gun cartridges. He gave me one as a present.

The idea was to let it off under Stacey's sun lounger whilst she slept but I'd forgotten, so now seemed the ideal opportunity. I told Heather what I was going to do and off I went sneaking up the stairs. Glancing down at the fuse I recalled asking Javier, "How long have I got once I've lit the fuse?" He had just shrugged his shoulders in response.

The storm had put everybody on edge so I knew a loud bang at this time of night would get the maximum response. I didn't think the joke was worth loosing my hand over, so I positioned the—I suppose you can only describe it as an explosive—on the steps near the top. I lit the fuse and waited.....

BANG!!!!!

Javier's had sounded 10 times times louder than your average banger, but this, with the echo caused by the house design, sounded 10 times times louder than Javier's. Stacey, Ashlie, and Scott ran out onto the landing, panicking. "What the hell was that?" They shouted in unison. "Funny," I thought, "that's just what I said when Javier had done it." In fact I only presumed that is what they said; in truth I was actually lip reading because I couldn't hear anything for 2 days. As Stacey turned the top of the steps she was met by the smell of gunpowder, a haze of smoke, and bits of paper floating down around me. I was wearing the same stupid grin Javier had, my left hand nursing my ear and a lighter in my right hand.

Stacey tutted loudly, shook her head and announced "It's like living in bloody Sharon Osborne's house."

"Yerrr mannn."

On the day of the bonfire we prepared the barbecue and down in Loja I bumped into Van Cleef at the butcher's. *"¡Para barbacoa!"* he shouted across the shop, holding up a large bag of meat.

"Why are you buying food for the barbecue? I will take care of that," I shouted back.

"I'm not eating your stuff!" came the reply I was half expecting.

Back at the house I spread the charcoal on our newly purchased barbecue and went to work starting to light it. Inside, the girls were busy making the traditional toffee, Heather was preparing the food, and Scott was putting anything and everything into a self-styled punch. Not having a punch bowl, we used a new washing-up bowl.

As people started to arrive, drinks were passed around and Van Cleef strolled over to where I was still trying to get the barbecue to light. *"¿Qué haces?"* What are you doing? he asked.

"Un fuego," a fire, I replied sarcastically. The shove on the arm I received must have left a bruise the size of a tennis ball. Once out of the way, he scraped all the charcoal I had been nursing for about half an hour to one side and replaced it with bits of wood. Within 5 minutes he had a roaring fire going. And within another 10, the embers were ready to accept food.

The punch, to my surprise, went down a storm, so as darkness fell everybody was in a merry mood. Unfortunately Fernando and his wife, Adori, had to leave to open the bar, so as we waved them off we all moved to the front of the house for the bonfire.

We hadn't really prepared anything, and as a result I just grabbed some firewood from the garage and set light to it. Some olive trees nearby had been trimmed so their branches went on as well. In the distance, Van Cleef and two of his sons could be seen dragging a couple of pallets. God only knows where they had come from.

Before we knew it there was a large fire burning. We all brought our chairs around from the back of the house to enjoy the warmth it gave out. Although it had been warm enough during the day to have a barbecue, at this time of year once the sun goes down it can get incredibly cold.

One of the girls appeared carrying the toffee they'd made in a large plastic container. As it was passed around, the Spanish looked on curiously as we, along with our English friends Jim and Diane, dived into the container and chewed away.

Encarna has always had a sweet tooth so she was the first to enquire what it was.

"Try it," I said. She picked out the smallest piece she could find, smelt it, licked it then popped it all in her mouth. She nodded her approval to the rest of the Spanish and they all moved forward for a piece. Throughout the rest of the night you could often hear the phrase *"¿Dónde esté el toffeeee?"* Where is the toffee? I'm sure it was only coincidence that a few weeks later Van Cleef had to have all his teeth taken out... or was it?

The smell of the toffee and the wood burning, along with the sound of people having a good time, reminded me of the bonfire nights I enjoyed as a kid. I sighed and said to Van Cleef that the only thing missing now is the pops, whizzing, and bangs of the fireworks. I'd said this almost to myself in English, so I can only presume that Van Cleef's grasp of our language is getting better.

BANG!

In an effort to make the night complete he had gone to his car, retrieved his shotgun, loaded it and fired it into the air, right behind my left ear. "Different," I said. "But not sure how it would have gone down in Leeds." I was also a little concerned about our telephone line, which ran above us.

Stacey ran over, nearly spilling the toffee. "What the hell was that?" I nodded toward the culprit. "I suppose it could have been worse; he might have just thrown a cartridge into the fire," I explained.

I'm sure I could see Stacey thinking, "God yes, we'd have all got covered in ink!"

As the night went on you would have expected the assembled crowd to diminish, but that wasn't the case. As people drove past on their way home from the bar, they would just pull over get out of their vehicles and join the party. It was almost 3am before the last person left with the shout, "Again next year!"

Scott and I often spent the morning playing tennis. Our village isn't very big but the facilities it does have are very good. It boasts its own tennis courts and football pitch, free for anybody to use. It was whilst walking back from one of these thrashings—yes, Scott won every time—that we bumped into Javier coming out of the bar. *"¡Miras!"* Look, he shouted as he beckoned us over to the back of his car.

In England you would expect the boot to be opened and a varied display of knocked off jeans and DVDs to greet you, but this is Spain. In the back were two massive, dead, wild boar. The fruits of a morning's hunting.

It was now the season to go boar hunting. I had already been invited to join them down on the farm, a phrase that for some reason conjured up my result on the Internet when searching for gout.

The invitation was to witness the killing of the boars they kept on the farms. This isn't carried out like it is back in the UK. There is no quick electrocution before a bolt through the head. Around here they just smack it over the head with a blunt instrument, quickly wrap a chain or some rope around its back feet, hoist it up then ram a sharp knife into its throat before dragging it all the way down its stomach.

"Thanks, but no thanks," had been my reply to the invitation.

Later that day Javier came over to the house; he had a candle burning for Stacey that was burning very brightly indeed. "Do you want to see the piglets? *Los bébes.*" Novel chat up line I thought. He would often call with such invitations. A couple of days ago it was to go and see his new foal. On this occasion the invitation was to all of us. Having nothing else to do, we agreed and followed him across the olive groves, looking as English as ever, including Scott in his England shorts and flip flops. We searched a couple of outhouses and eventually found a large shed with a bolted and locked door. *"¡En aquí!"* In here, he stated proudly. He unlocked the door and as he slid the bolt back we crowded around with anticipation. The mother turned and stared at us. It wasn't one of the docile pink pigs you find at the local urban farm, no, this was the size of a Shetland pony, covered in dark coarse hair. It was a female wild boar. Thankfully the females don't have the large, menacing tusks that the males have, just a smaller version. Nevertheless we all took a step back.

"What can it do?" asked Heather. "It can only give you a nasty nudge." The piglets did look rather cute but the mother herded them into a corner away from us. We had seen what we had come to see and were about to walk away when Javier said, "*Un momento*," and crouched by the door. As the mother approached he picked up a small stone and threw it at her head. She snorted and backed off.

A more naïve one of the piglets advanced curiously. Javier grabbed its leg and dragged it out, managing to slam the door just as the mother came forward. He held the small creature up and we all gathered around and stroked it. As it squealed I could see the door banging over Javier's shoulder. I was comforted by the phrase, "It can only give you a nasty nudge."

Eventually Javier turned with the intention of reuniting mother and baby. As he opened the door the mother showed just why they are called WILD BOARS. It charged forward. Heather's natural, motherly instincts kicked in. She pushed Ashlie out of the way and ran like hell. Ashlie regained her composure and began searching for something to climb. Scott's little white legs were a blur as he scurried across the yard kicking up a mini dust devil behind him. Stacey disappeared without a trace. Personally, I tried to display a little more composure by retreating from the scene by running backwards. It was only when I thought that I may need a little more distance between me and the creature that I realised I had run backwards into a corner and had nowhere to go. When I looked back at the outhouse door I could see the boar was trying to take a chunk out of Javier's leg, and he was trying frantically to kick the animal with his other leg and beat it with his fists. Just as I was about to go and rescue him (honest) he gave it an almighty kick and forced it back into the shed.

I asked him how he was and he tried to brush the whole incident off, although I could see blood on his hand. He was leaning against the shed door and looking around on the floor. "What are you looking for?" I asked.

"*Las llaves*." The keys, he replied.

Scott strolled up and said. "You threw them and the bolt inside at the boar when you were fighting it." There was nothing else for it; he had to go back in.

As he opened the door the boar made a break for freedom. We all ran again, back to our hiding places. Knowing that Javier didn't need rescuing this time I retreated to more open ground.

After retrieving the bolt and keys, off Javier went to round up the mother. His expression read "f****ing English." Ten minutes later all was well with the world and we all walked back to our house, or in Javier's case, limped. I asked on several occasions later how his leg was but he just kept repeating, "*No problema.*"

You can imagine our hesitation when a week later Javier invited all of us to his farm again and muttered something about wild boar.

Sunday arrived and we waited with bated breath. Eventually Javier pulled up and tooted the horn of his Land Rover; it was 2:30pm. I looked at Ashlie, Heather, and Scott and thought to myself, "Once more unto the breach." Or something like that. Ashlie turned and asked, "Where exactly are we going and what are we doing when we get there?" I explained that this was a common occurrence over here in Spain and if I had a Euro for every time I went on one of these 'mystery tours' then I would be a very wealthy ex-pat.

We all climbed into the car and 10 minutes later we pulled up at Javier's family farm. Although most of the animals are kept there, only Javier's brother, Fermin, actually lives there. So I was a little surprised to see about half a dozen cars outside.

We parked up and went in to be greeted by Javier's complete family including cousins.

Inside, the house was like a throw back from the 1950s, complete with plastic covered suite. In the centre were three small tables with plates of various meats. In the open hearth on a roaring fire was a pan full of chopped meat. It was then explained that after hunting down the boars the other day (the ones I saw in the back of the car when I was expecting jeans & DVDs) they had been carved up, and in front of us now was just a small section of the prepared carcass.

Cans of beer were shoved in our hands along with forks, and for the next 2 hours we were almost force-fed. Ashlie's face was a picture; you would think the food had been prepared by a KGB chef for a rebellious dissident spy. Fortunately Scott eats almost anything so he was nominated to try and clear the plates that were put in front of us, but even for Scott this was quite a formidable task.

I'm not sure if it was the beer or the food but Scott let one go. (What is it with people when they come over here?) It crossed my mind that if anybody noticed I would explain that this was the equivalent of the Arabs burping after a meal… simply a display of appreciation. Alas, it went unnoticed.

The plates of food diminished and Javier's mother came in from the kitchen and asked if anyone wanted a coffee. "I think it's coming to an end," I said noting the time to be 5pm. Wrong. Along with the coffee came the buns, cakes, etc, etc. After we had finished these we were offered, and tried, the red wine, the sherry, and the port. We then, and when I say "we," I mean everybody, not just the alcoholic English, went on to the whiskey and Bacardi.

At 7pm it was suggested we all retire to the bar. I went to the toilet, came out, and went over to Javier's car. The door was locked so I banged on the window. He reached over and flicked the door lock. As I climbed in I jokingly asked, "Why the locks, are there thieves around here?" I then noticed I was not next to Javier. I had got in the wrong car.

At the bar the rest of the locals joined us. Van Cleef was sitting nearby. He had been hunting all day and in front of him, on the bar, was one of his trophies, a boar's tail—very hygienic.

They say try everything once, which I heartedly agree with and often do, but when we got the invite to repeat last week again I was caught off guard, again, and for some reason out came the words. "We'd love to" when what I had meant to say was, "No thanks."

So there we all were back at the farmhouse just like last week. As before, we were greeted with a beer, and seated between an open fire and a table containing an assortment of meats. Within 10 minutes the Spanish women were congregating discussing wifey-things. The Spanish men sat huddled together talking about shooting, and we, the English, sat prodding and poking food trying to guess not only what part of the animal it was but also which animal it came from.

After the meat came the cheese… then the bread… then …the ammunition. Yes, we all got to look at the cartridges used that morning. To me the only difference was the colour, but I seemed to nod in the right places. Then out came the guns and the men moved outside. It was suggested that Scott follow with his camera.

One of the men present stood in a shooting jacket with a dozen birds and 4 rabbits hanging limply from each side. He stood in a shooting pose and waited for his picture to be taken. Somebody then suggested that I should have my picture taken, so off came his jacket and with the help of three of the men, I was bundled into it and a shotgun was thrust into my hand. It was difficult trying to pose and stop the blood from going all over my clean trousers.

A pigeon landed with a thud nearby as its migration was cut abruptly short. A small cheer went up and the man who shot it went to recover his trophy. *"¿Quieres probar Allaaan?"* Do I want a go? Why not?

Now it's always been a bit of a standing joke in the village that in our house everything in the kitchen comes from tins. No decapitating or plucking for Heather.

So when it was suggested I aim for a can about 50 yards away, and not anything that actually breathes, I wasn't surprised.

Bang!

A direct hit. Well, we'll never go hungry again. I can always nip out into the *campo* and hunt down a wild tin if necessary.

So back in the house the coffee was served and cleared away and somebody asked if I wanted a Bacardi. Experience told me that this was a natural progression and before long everybody would be joining in. The man who asked me went to a cupboard, pulled out a bottle with Arabic writing on it and shrugged his shoulders. I took this to mean this was all they had so I nodded back. After accepting half a pint of this beverage I returned to my seat. It was drinkable but only just. Then out came the Napoleon Brandy and the malt whiskey. I may have been a trifle premature in my choice.

Two hours later we all retired to the Fernando's bar. As the clock turned 12am, we went home, sick to death of alcohol and vowing not to drink again for a week. No problem, the only thing we have planned is to go and watch young Fernando play football for Loja in the morning. Young Fernando had played for Loja's football team for a several years. Loja are a 3rd division team, probably equivalent to somewhere like Blackpool in the English league.

We had overslept and were all taken by surprise when Van Cleef rang our doorbell and informed us that everybody else was waiting for us outside the bar. We got ready as fast as we could. Heather and I jumped into his car and Ash and Scott jumped into Javier's. Stacey didn't fancy it and decided to stay at home.

I won't go into details; but it would be adequate to say Loja won, which to be honest makes a change. "Well that was nice....back home now?" Wrong! We all stopped off at a bar on the way back for an hour. Then home? NO. After that everybody went to Santa Barbara where a fiesta was still going on. We went into the tent to find over 200 people getting ready to play bingo, so we bought our cards.

It all looked quite impressive; they even had a computer linked to a speaker system. Unfortunately when it started there was the imitation sound of twirling balls, then the first number was called. It sounded like a retarded 8-year-old girl on helium. Not one person could understand her. Every 2 minutes people were asking for a complete check. In the end we gave in and retired to the bar. Then home? NO.

Javier had left early, leaving Ashlie and Scott without a lift, and Van Cleef had offered somebody else a lift back to the village so space was limited. The girls all squeezed into the back and Scott and I ended up in the boot. I'm sure we went the longest and bumpiest way home.

Back at the village we were ushered into Pepe's bar for a final coffee. Then home? NO.

Fernando opened his bar and on we went to play dominos; Ashlie and Scott sloped off. Now one thing I forgot to mention earlier on the subject of dominoes is that if you ever play with somebody from Spain, take a book because they take more time to make a move than a Russian intellectual in a chess tournament.

At 10pm we made our excuses and left and went home. We aren't going to drink all this week...oh my god it's Christmas in less than 2 weeks... then New Year. I had planned a trip back to the UK in the New Year. I wondered if I could squeeze in a detox session while I'd be there.

Stacey, Ashlie, and Scott had all been searching for work over the last few weeks, but the lack of jobs and their limited Spanish was making it very difficult. Stacey was thinking about moving back to the UK, whilst Scott and Ashlie were talking about looking for work on the coast, where the language barrier isn't so much a problem.

Whilst looking through the *situations vacant* section in various free papers available on the coast, I came across the horoscopes in the magazine *The Sentinella*. Reading horoscopes is something I just never do, but these were just too spookily accurate to ignore.

Ashlie's TAURUS

Use your head this month when it comes to anything to do with Scooby Doo.

How weird is that because Scott, her boyfriend, has the nickname Scooby Doo. Read on...

Stacey's GEMINI

You will have a recurring nightmare that a snake is in your bed.

Could this have anything to do with her date that didn't work out recently?

Heather's PISCES

You have developed an annoying habit of snoring... loudly. For this reason you may find you are kicked out of bed so get used to the sofa.

Heather has been suffering from a cold and blocked nose, and snores all night, and that's when she isn't coughing. "My God," I thought, the writer of this is psychic.

Pam's AQUARIUS

Your other half is feeling generous and may feel like splashing the cash on you. Take advantage of this rare opportunity.

Now this is really getting spooky because Pam's boyfriend Gavin has just sold his house and taken her to New York.

Hang on, what does mine say????

Alan's LEO

Who ate all the pies? Who ate all the pies? You ate all the pies! You ate all the pies!

I told you horoscopes are a load of bollocks!

I showed Ashlie and Scott an advertisement in the same magazine asking for recruits at a large estate agent in Marbella.

After a short phone call both were offered an interview. The next day we all drove down to the head office and waited for 2 hours while the interviews took place.

Two days later they received a call saying they had both been successful, with Ashlie offered a position in the office and Scott in the sales department. The only problem was that they started on the 7th of January; not much time to find accommodations.

The discussion about getting a dog hasn't developed any further. Heather is still putting her foot down. Unfortunately for Heather so is my old buddy Van Cleef. "*No problema*," he says with a wink. Again he mimes bringing the dog to our house, sliding it through the gates, and ringing the bell. "*Papá Noel*," is the only word he says. I'm not convinced Heather will believe Father Christmas brought it.

Sitting in the square one day I noticed that the Sierra Nevada now had its caps covered by thick snow. Although we were about 50 miles away, they could be seen as clear as day. I pointed them out to Heather and reminded her of our little expedition during last May. She cringed and started biting her nails.

It all started during a conversation with some Brits we met. They explained how they had just come down from the Sierra Nevada. I asked what was up there at this time of the year (May) and they had described that, although almost everything is closed, it's a wonderful place to go for a walk and enjoy a coffee. So the very next day we decided to give it a go.

Once there we parked the car in the large underground car park and a minute later we were in the ski village; in fact we were the only ones in the ski village. Like they said, almost everything was closed and the only people about were a few workmen. It was difficult to imagine the hustle and bustle that would take over when the first snow arrives each year.

We had a coffee and bought a ticket for the gondola that would take us up to the ski area and more restaurants. It was a nice trip up and once there we were definitely the only people about. Stepping off the gondola the weather was much cooler and the breeze was welcoming. Then Heather noticed a ski lift that could take you to the top of the mountain, the kind that was a steel chair suspended by a simple steel rod. Now anybody that knows Heather will be aware of the nervous shakes she gets when anybody mentions anything to do with skiing. Although we have been on several ski holidays and had visited Sheffield dry ski centre numerous times, she becomes quite withdrawn, a little moody and slightly irritable, just at the thought of it. I think she thought it would be safe visiting the resort in spring, but the sight of this lift brought on all the above emotions. Of course, I suggested taking the chair to the top while Heather tried to convince me that our gondola tickets didn't cover us for this chair lift.

After a short conversation with the operator he grabbed one of the chairs for us to climb on, and off we went. Halfway up Heather asked, "How do we get off?"

"Just as you do when you have skis on," I replied, "No forget that," I added as I recalled that Heather's usual style of exit was to wait until the chair had reached the top, lift the safety bar, push the passengers either side out of the way, dive off, land flat on her face and start screaming. "I can't get up, I'm stuck and I'm gonna get squashed by the next chair....I'M GOING TO DIE! HEEEELLLLPPPP!!"

Having arrived wearing only t-shirts we were now at about 8,000ft and still climbing. Our chair was swinging in a freezing breeze and we were wrong about there being no snow. Even though it was May and 37 degrees when we left our house, we now had snowdrifts passing under our feet.

Heather's problems disembarking were easily solved. It was so bloody cold we sat tight while the chair swung around the large cogged wheel at the top, waved to the operator who had come out of his little hut to help us off, and were on our way back down again.

At the bottom, the original operator smiled and stopped the lift to let us off. I'm sure I saw a twinkle in his eye and a knowing smirk at the side of his mouth at our hasty return. Next time it's winter woollies for us.

Back in the Square, Van Cleef's son, Raul, joined in the conversation we were having about skiing. "*Un momento,*" he said and disappeared down the street. He returned 5 minutes later with a pair of carver skis complete with bindings. He offered them to me with a smile. I explained that I had hinted to Heather that something similar would be very nice for Christmas. Unfortunately as they cost at least €300 (£200) I wasn't holding my breath.

"*Un regalo para ti,*" a present for you, he said.

"But they're yours," he went on to explain how he had tried it for a day and hadn't enjoyed it so didn't need them anymore.

"Why did you buy them?" I asked. He held out his right hand extended his fingers and closed them fluently, one finger at a time starting with his little finger. This I had previously learned is the Andalucian hand sign for taking something without the expressed permission of the owner and without any due intention to return them to the said owner. In other words, he nicked them!

"*Dos años pasado,*" 2 years ago, he said with a smirk. Not one to look a gift horse in the mouth I said all I need now are the poles. He patted me on the back and said.

"*No problema,*" and repeated the hand gesture again.

"No, no, no," I said interrupting him quickly. "Red please."

Chapter 18
It's Christmas!

One of the main reasons for moving to Spain was for the nice, warm weather, and what do we get? A WHITE CHRISTMAS! Yes, as I write this we are surrounded by mountains where the snow is settling and, get this, at night it goes down to –5 degrees. As we only have the coal fire in the front room for heating, it's absolutely freezing.

Stacey was being helpful the other day and had decided to hang out the washing. At lunch time Heather went out to check how well it was drying. She was amazed to find that it was all completely dry, all within an hour? We then realised that the washer had never been turned on. Stacey didn't even realise the clothes weren't damp when she hung them out.

Speaking of Stacey's faux pas... After reflecting on the conversation she had overheard us having a few days ago, about the high quantity of suicides in the village, she asked out of the blue, "How often do people kill themselves in this village?"

"Only the once," I replied.

I think I may have mentioned that I have an ambition. One day I want to become the village *Presidente*. Well, as they say over here, *poco, poco* (little by little). So when it was suggested I play the part of the 'Black' king in the Jan 5th, three kings parade I took it as a compliment, although dressing up as Al Jolson seemed a long way from being inaugurated as '*El Presidente.*' Unfortunately

I will be back in the UK so had to decline the offer. The next thing I know I am in the bar being presented with a Santa suit. Tomorrow, Christmas Eve, I am the village Santa. I'm sure I have a case for victimization.

I've just opened the last door on the advent calendar and it was a Santa. With political correctness in the UK it would have probably been a multi coloured snowperson. After devouring the chocolate I tossed the box into the fire. You would have thought I had tarred and feathered Santa before cutting off his beard and serving Rudolf for Christmas dinner. Heather went mental, claiming that as part of the decorations the calendar should have stayed up until the 12th night.... She's not speaking to me at the moment.

As night time approached I donned the Father Christmas suit I'd been given and had the traditional sherry. Also getting into the spirit of things, Heather, Stacey, and Ashlie decorated some 'Johnny Walker' hats they'd acquired from somewhere with silver foil, tinsel, and the odd Christmas tree baubles, and put on some t-shirts with Rudolph on them. To cap it all they added the essential antlers to the tops of their heads. Scott dressed up in sun glasses, Bermuda shorts, and Hawaiian shirt... Doesn't everybody?

We had no idea what to expect when we entered the bar. Fernando and Adori seemed quite proud of their single star and the free cardboard Coca-Cola Christmas tree; these were the total sum of the bar's decorations.

We entered and shouted, *"¡Feliz Navidad!"* and a few people groaned what I accepted to be the same in reply. As I looked around, the atmosphere was not what you would expect to find in a British pub on Christmas Eve. Of course the fact that in Spain presents are exchanged on the 5th of January may have had something to do with it.

As well as the suit and the oversized white beard I had also put sunglasses on to hide my identity from the young; I didn't want to shatter any elusions. Upon entering I noticed they were all sitting at the same table, so I approached with a "Ho Ho Ho!"

"Allaaan," they shouted in unison. So much for the disguise.

Stacey had thrown caution and her straighteners to the wind and decided to go out with her hair curled tonight. Javier entered the bar and joined us at our table. I saw him staring at Stacey, which to be honest wasn't unusual, but then he called her name. As she turned to face him he pointed at her hair, made some kind of grunting noise and pulled a face.

"Javier!" I said.

"*¿Qué?*" what, he asked.

"You need to learn some tact."

"*¿Qué?*" he repeated.

"If a lady has changed her hair style and you don't like it, you still say it's nice."

"*¿Porqué?*" Why? he asked. I knew I was on a losing ticket with this because I had had a similar conversation with Encarna a few weeks ago. At the time, we were sitting and talking when Diane came across and gave Heather a piece of paper. "*¿Qué es?*" What is that? Encarna had asked. Heather explained that it was a diet sheet she had asked Diane to copy for her. Encarna had waved her arms around shouting that Heather didn't need to diet. She then looked at the Spanish woman to her left and announced. "Now she needs to diet!" The poor woman just stared at her own midriff.

I think the Spanish would do great on the TV programme *Catch Phrase*. As I remember, all you had to do was "Say what you see!"

As the night wore on, people began to relax and let their hair down a bit. At one stage there was a small queue of people, male and female, waiting to sit on my knee to have their photographs taken with Santa, and none of them were under the age of 40.

The night inevitably ended up with a game of bingo. Every time number 25 was called, we, as in us Brits, all stood up and sang the first verse of, "We Wish You a Merry Christmas," then sat down as though nothing had happened. I think some of the Spanish were debating whether or not to call the men in the white coats.

The next morning Ashlie got everybody up at 7:30 to open our presents (even though we didn't get to bed until 5am.) Heather said, "I think it's time we tell her Santa doesn't exist." What does she mean he doesn't exist?

We all opened our presents and nobody was disappointed. Heather, in an effort to stop Raul from doing jail time, had got me the ski poles I needed, and for the rest of the morning the air smelled of new perfumes, and people danced in front of the mirror trying on new clothes.

Javier called in later and nearly had an orgasm over the new mobile phone we had clubbed together to buy him. The phone was a thank you for the help he had given Scott and the girls. Since they had arrived he'd introduced them to all the other young ones in the village and taken them all to the discos on several occasions.

Between Christmas and the New Year was the only time available to find Ashlie and Scott somewhere to live in Marbella. So off we went, unfortunately to one of the most expensive places in Spain to rent. As the jobs they had were in the centre and buying transport was out of the question, expectations were somewhat low.

The first apartment we looked at was minute and filthy and €800 (£550) a month.

The 2nd estate agent sounded more hopeful but when we arrived at the apartment the stupid woman had the wrong key. This was the pattern throughout the day. Then we found one that wasn't too bad, a one bedroom in the centre—again at €800, plus a 2 month deposit. And get this, over here YOU have to pay one month as commission for the estate agent. As a last resort we thought we would try one more. The estate agent said we couldn't all fit in the car so Heather went with Ashlie and Scott. When they returned they were all beaming. The last one had been the best by far. At €700 a month, with only one month's deposit and only half a month's commission, a deal was clinched and a deposit was put down. We get rid of them....I mean they move out next Tuesday.

Chapter 19
An Accident Waiting to Happen

Stacey wanted to go skiing before returning to the UK and as she was going back on the 5th of January, New Years' Eve was the only day available. Ashlie and Scott had their packing to do so it was only to be Heather, Stacey, and myself. "Get all your gear ready because we need an early start," I said.

We were warned it would be busy so we were up at 6:30am. Heather and Stacey spent the next 15 minutes looking for hats, gloves, and scarves. So much for getting everything ready.

At last we were off and because it was Sunday, as well as New Years' Eve, the roads were quiet. Arriving at the top of the mountain we found out why. Every man and his dog in Spain was there, all queuing for this and that. It was only 8:45am.

We parked the car and decided to do a toilet stop first, personally this entailed taking off about 4 layers of clothing to get down to the braces on my salopets. Ten minutes later and back at the car, I realised I had lost my hat, so back to the toilets—nothing there.

Never mind, off we went. "Just a minute," Heather said, "I've lost a glove." We spent the next 10 minutes looking for her glove to no avail. We left the car park and went to hire the skis and boots. The woman in the shop asked if we had our lift passes yet. When we said no she suggested we get them ASAP as they only had a limited number. At the kiosk we were told there weren't any all-day passes left, only 1pm-5pm. We had come this far so we bought those and went back to the hire centre. The saleswoman explained we would still need to hire the equipment for the full day, so we did and took it all to the car rather than carry it around all morning.

After we had loaded it into the boot, I said. "Oh, I can't find my scarf." At this point Stacey decided to make sure it wasn't round my neck. As she went to grab the collar of my jacket I turned around. I can only presume it was her fingernail that gouged a chunk out of my ear. There was blood everywhere. Stacey went to the toilet for some tissue, whilst I had to hold my head out to stop the blood from going all over my jacket; it was dripping all over the floor.

Outside the cold stemmed the blood flow, and it was then I realised I'd lost my sunglasses. Heather needed to replace her gloves so we approached a man selling ski paraphernalia at a stall in the village square. She tried a few on and decided on the pair she liked best. We bought them. She'd only tried one on. When she put on the other she found the thumb on it had been sewn closed. Back we went to swap them.

Because we had a few hours to kill we thought we'd have sandwiches. We settled down and asked the approaching waitress for three Cokes and two chicken, tomato, and lettuce sandwiches, as described in the menu. They arrived with chips, which was an added bonus. As we tasted the sandwiches we all looked at each other; they were disgusting. Inside was some kind of mayonnaise mixed with coleslaw and a few other unidentifiable ingredients. After double-checking the menu it appeared that the waitress had brought us the vegetarian option. (How the hell you veggies eat this stuff I don't know!) After complaining, she eventually brought us our original order.

The gondola queue looked like it would take about an hour to go down, so I suggested getting our skis on early and joining the queue at about 12 o'clock. By the time we were ready the line of people had reduced, and before we knew it we were climbing the mountain.

As I mentioned before, Heather is famed for her pre-skiing nerves. By now her fingernails were down to her knuckles and any question asked was returned with a short, snappy answer. We all agreed that a trip down a green run (very easy) was in order. Stacey was the first to fall.

For the next few hours everything was going great—that was until Heather fell halfway down a steep blue run. (Not so easy.) I waited at the bottom and watched whilst Stacey retrieved Heather's lost ski and tried to help her put it back on. I was out of earshot but I could guess the conversation. It probably went something like this...

STACEY: Come on mum, are you okay?

HEATHER: Whose bloody idea was it to come down this run? I bet it was yer father's. Well I won't be able to get that bloody thing back on, this hill's too steep. I'll take the other off and go down on my arse.

STACEY: You can't do that, somebody will hit you.

HEATHER: (Sounding like Dick Dastardly's dog, Muttley) Nassum fassum fissum etc, etc, etc.

Five minutes later they both came down on skis. I asked what had happened and Stacey relayed the conversation on the hill exactly as I had described above.

Everything was going well and after a coffee we all agreed to ski the whole way down. About 2/3 of the way I hit a bump. You know what's coming next don't you?

I went up in the air and came down awkwardly. The pain was unbelievable; it felt like a shark was hanging from my left calf. Heather and Stacey skied down to me and asked how I was. "In agony!" I replied, bottom lip trembling. I managed to get back on my skis and fumbled with my poles to try and complete the rest of the run.

As the hill got steeper and my speed increased I realised I hadn't the strength in my bad leg to turn. I tried, but once again down I went, arse over...well, you know. (Later Stacey said I had looked like Bridget Jones going down the slope.)

A couple of young Spanish girls retrieved my skis and asked if I was okay. I smiled up at them and said, "Sí, muy bien." As they left, my bottom lip regained its tremor as I realised I had caused exactly the same injury to my other leg. Somehow, probably because I'm a man, I was able to climb back on my skis and finish the other 200 metres to the bottom.

I took off my skis as Heather and Stacey joined me and I announced, "I can't walk!" They got me to a chair, took my skis back to the car, and brought me my shoes. I suggested they return their hired skis whilst I stumbled to the car park. By the time they had returned them, even though there was a queue, I had only walked 50 metres.

Eventually I made it to the car and Heather drove us all home. We were due to go to the bar to celebrate New Year. Obviously the rest of the family didn't want to go without me so I was given 2 extra strong Paracetomol, a codeine tablet, and a triple whiskey. What a caring family I have.

The Spanish have a funny way of celebrating New Year. Everybody goes to the bar. Then at 10:30 everybody goes home for a family meal and to eat 12 grapes as the clock chimes in the New Year. At 12:30 everybody returns to the bar.

At the bar we were invited to stay and have a meal with Fernando's and Van Cleef's families. We all downed copious amounts of wine, Bacardi, whiskey, and sherry. I wasn't exactly drunk, just spaced out of my tiny mind.

At 2am Heather and I decided to go. Van Cleef had been told about my injury so offered to help me walk out and drive me home (it was only about 100 yards up the road). Because I couldn't put any weight on my legs, Van Cleef had to virtually carry me. At the door he turned and announced in very loud Spanish, "I have to take the English man home because he is pissed out of his head."

The next day Heather took me down to the local hospital where I was given a thorough examination, an injection for the pain, and some more tablets. Apparently I had torn all the calf muscles in both legs. I blame the knocked off skis.

Once I'm okay I'm straight back up that mountain…

Well I think I will have to stop there for a while, my tablet or is it tabletsssssss hhhaavve kihckked IIIiiinnnnnnnnnnnnnnnnnnnn . . .

Chapter 20
The Price You Pay

Well, Ashlie and Scott were shipped off to sunny Marbella, where they are now busily grafting away.

Stacey and I were to fly back to the UK. She was to stay at Pamela's house, and after speaking to her old employer had secured her old job back. Her long term plan was to complete the course, TEAFL, teaching English as a foreign language, then return to Spain in a year's time as a missionary, teaching people like Van Cleef the Queen's English. Yer, fat chance. I mean converting Van Cleef, not completing the course.

My reason for a trip back to the UK was to see my father, who, I found out having spoken to my mother, had taken a turn for the worse.

Whilst waiting at the airport I let Stacey do all the queuing since I still had my skiing injury. I sat reading my book when a small Asian boy about 8 years old stopped and stared at the seat next to me. He looked under and over it before his mother and father joined him. "But it was here... I left it for only a minute." I saw him earlier, playing with a new Nintendo DS game machine. His mother said, "Well it's gone now, that will teach you a little responsibility."

The young lad looked at me, near to tears, and asked, "Have you seen my DS mister?" With a lump in my throat I asked him how long ago he'd left it.

"Just a couple of seconds," he said searching under the chair for the tenth time. I turned to the mother and explained that I had only been sitting there a couple of minutes and had seen nothing. The child's mother smiled and, out of view of her son, mouthed the words. "I've got it." I was astonished; the child was beside himself. I said to her, "This reminds me of the time my wife bought me a £400 leather jacket, a couple of weeks later we were in a pub and I put my jacket on a chair. When I turned around it was gone. Inside I hoped my wife had hidden it to teach me a lesson."

The woman smiled, "And had she?"

"No, somebody had stolen it."

The woman frowned and said, "Oooh dear."

I continued. "So I know exactly how that kid feels at the moment." I then added with a smile, "You're a cruel, unfit mother." She smiled and a couple of minutes later they all boarded the plane. She still hadn't told him. My guess? That kid's going to get a Nintendo DS for his next birthday…the cheap skates.

The plane left Granada for Liverpool and as a distraction I ordered a drink and was given a bag of whiskey—that's right, a bag of whiskey. (Two in fact, as they were on special offer). I can only assume that miniature bottles can be used to break down the security door and hold the pilot for ransom. Oh yes, I forgot to mention, I was stopped at security after the x-ray of my hand luggage showed I had smuggled 300ml of shaving foam and the maximum allowance was 100ml. So once I've smashed my miniature bottle and threatened the pilot I am going to relieve him of his moustache and sideburns. God, I'm surprised they let me on board!

Two and a half hours later we landed at Liverpool—well I thought we had, but once off the plane we had several hundred yards to walk. In fact, it was so far I considered asking for a rebate on some of my fare.

I am often asked if there is anything I miss out in Spain. Well yes there is, besides the family of course. GREGGS' STEAK BAKES! For the uninitiated, these pastries from paradise should be recognised as one of the 7 wonders of the world. They are absolutely fantastic, and there is only one way to eat them—with a sausage roll.

I was in the UK for 5 days and I had both steak bake and sausage roll for lunch everyday. Jesus wept did I have heart burn by the time I went back. My trip should have been sponsored by 'Rennie'.

The first thing I did on arrival was to go and visit my father. He looked a lot worse than the last time I saw him, if that was possible. Having spent only a few hours with him I began to realise just how difficult it must be for my mother. To see the person you have spent your entire life with literally dying before your eyes must be like somebody wrenching your heart out. He slept most of the time and when he was awake it was difficult to understand him. But like last time, he tried to sustain his humour, explaining how he thought all the nurses at the hospital fancied him. He finished with a wink and the phrase, "I've still got it."

I'd promised to meet up with our old neighbours once again. So off we went for another Chinese meal. We sat and bitched about the people who bought our house and generally chewed the fat. I was then asked what we do with our time in Spain. I explained about my 4-minute record for holding my breath under water, something I'd built up over time. Then, as an example of how I spend my time, I relayed the problem we had had with the pool last year. We had found black bits on the pool floor one day. The only way to remove them was to scrub them. As the pool has a depth of 1.5 metres (all over) it had to be done under water. Yes, I can hold my breath for 4 minutes, but only whilst floating on top. The area around the steps was easy because I could hook my feet under them.

Actually taking a gulp of air, diving down and scrubbing was out of the question. I needed to be held down. I filled a bucket with rocks, placed it in the water, swam down, and hooked my arm into it. Better, but I needed to be under for longer. "The garden hose!" I thought. Picture this, it's more amusing: I placed a peg on my nose, put the garden hose in my mouth, jumped in with the hand brush, and started scrubbing. Now I'm sure there's a physics teacher out there who could explain why I nearly drowned. It's probably something to do with the pressure in the hose. Anyway, it was back to the drawing board. Thirty minutes later I had fastened

2 hand brushes to my flip flops and for the rest of the day I walked up and down the pool. Job done.

The friends I was dining with just looked at me, and eventually one said, "Alan, you need a hobby."

On my last day I made sure Stacey was settled in, then before heading out to the airport called once again at my mother's. "I'm sorry," she said. "Your dad's in bed asleep."

"That's okay, don't wake him," I said. We had a cup of tea and again I made her promise to phone if either of them needed me. As I left I had a sick feeling in my stomach.

It was one week later at 3 o'clock in the morning when I got the phone call. My father had once again been taken to hospital after collapsing. The doctors told my mother to expect the worst. She immediately rang my brothers and sister who all arrived just as he passed away. Only minutes before, he was apologising to everybody for the inconvenience he was putting them all through.

When you make the decision to move abroad you subconsciously know that there is every possibility that you will miss out on moments such as this. Being the only member of the family not to be at the bedside is something I will have to live with for the rest of my life, or as they say, "the price you pay."

My sister rang again the next day to explain that the funeral could not be held for another two weeks. Why? Because it was a busy time of the year. When I explained this to my friends in the village they couldn't believe it, thinking they had misunderstood me. "Everybody here is buried within two days," they would say. "Paco in the next village was buried the same day," says another. I was a little embarrassed how we do things back in the UK.

Heather, Ashlie, and I all flew back to attend the funeral. My mother asked me if I wanted to go to the funeral director's to see my dad one last time. I agreed and Heather tactfully declined.

It was the first time I'd been inside a funeral director's and certainly the first time I had seen a dead body. As we entered, the smell and the feeling were somewhat familiar. Then I remembered walking behind Van Cleef whilst hunting.

The staff was very pleasant and my mother let me go in by myself whilst she waited outside. My dad was laid in the coffin wearing his favourite suit and even his flat cap. He had a smile to the side of his mouth that reminded me of David Jason playing

'Dell boy' in '*Only Fools and Horses*.' I smiled at the thought, bent down and kissed his forehead. "Sleep tight," I said, and then left before the sadness returned.

The funeral, like any other, is a difficult time for family and friends. My sister had agreed to do a small speech. Throughout it she mentioned my father's youth, his eleven brothers and sisters, and his time in the Navy. On several occasions her voice broke with sorrow. I remember at the time wondering where she had gotten the strength, knowing that I couldn't have stood in front of everybody, looking over my father's coffin and joking about the time he was evacuated during the war and only moved 3 miles down the road. "He would often go home for his tea," she added.

Although I knew my mother missed my father immensely, I couldn't help thinking that his passing had been some kind of release for her. She once mentioned to me that one of the first things she did when she woke up in a morning was check to see if my father, lying next to her, was still alive.

A few days later and we were back on a plane to Spain. We explained to my mother that we would be returning in a month's time and on that occasion when we went back to Spain we would take her back with us for a holiday.

The same morning that my father died, one of Van Cleef's other dogs had had puppies. I think the fact I was feeling rather down swayed Heathers vote on the 'get dog, not get dog' debate, and before we knew it we were down at his house choosing one. Van Cleef wasn't there but his wife Encarna was happy to help. That makes her sound like an assistant at ASDA doesn't it? "*¿Cuál?*" Which? she asked. There were five to choose from, all different in their own way. "I don't mind," I said, "as long as it's male." Eventually we chose a white one with a brown ring on its tail and matching brown ears. Its stomach was covered in brown spots. "A Dalmatian in the family I think," I said as Encarna dragged it from the kennel. I asked, "That one is male, isn't it?" She turned it over, pointed to a protruding part of its anatomy and said, "*¡Claro!*" Of course!

We e-mailed all our friends, as we do every couple of weeks just to let them know what we are doing. I thought it would be fun to include a name-that-dog competition and attached some photos of the new addition to the family. The favourite name up until then had been '*Copito*' which means snowflake.

A couple of days later I was teasing the puppy in front of the fire Javier called. Like most Spanish, he regards all animals as animals, and finds the way we deal with animals as part of the family a completely alien concept. Nevertheless, he joined in rolling the puppy onto its back. "*¿Qué se llama?*" What is it called? he asked. I explained about the naming competition I had e-mailed our friends, and then I added, "I quite like the name, *Copito*."

Javier thought for a while and then asked, "*Es Copita, no Copito.*" The difference being a male's name would end in an 'O' and a female's name would end in an 'A'.

We both looked down at the puppy that was still on its back rolling back and forward. I asked the question I wasn't sure I wanted the answer to. "*Este perro es macho, ¿no?*"

He looked at me as though I had two heads. He then pointed between the dog's legs, raised his eyebrows and tilted his head to one side. Not a word was said but he was shouting at me, "Are you blind?"

"I'll kill Encarna . Another bloody female in the house!" I got the computer out and sent the following e-mail:

E-MAIL
TO: FRIENDS AND FAMILY
FROM: CUTHBERTSONS
Hi gang.
Well we have a bit of bad news....

My new baby, the son I've waited for so long (I'm talking about my new dog, I'm not including Digby, the cat, as a son because Stacey's mollycoddling has made him as macho as Graham Norton) has a medical problem. . . . He's got a tuppence.

Yes my son is a daughter . . . another bloody woman in the house, as if we don't have enough already. I've yet to take this matter up with Van Cleef the village baby dealer. He did assure me that it was a male and Encarna his wife also checked when I asked again on collection.

I have considered returning 'her' and asking for the male I desired in exchange, but apparently this is frowned upon . . . or it was at the Clarendon wing back in the mid 80s when we had Stacey and Ashlie.

So as it stands we now have to spend the next 6 months walking around the village with a big stick keeping all the randy Spanish dogs at bay….. a little bit like we did when Stacey and Ashlie were over here. The last thing I want is puppies all over the place, I think even Digby and Ollie would draw the line at that.

With regards the naming competition, it's back on. The only difference is we are now looking for a feminine one.

Stacey's suggestion when hearing the news . . . 'TUPPENCE'

Got to go now….. Ollie's just gobbed on her new sister.

Casa Cuthies

In the end I had to cancel the competition, almost everybody came up with the same suggestion…. FANNY. We did consider naming her Jesus, after finding her walking across the swimming pool. Thank God I'd put the cover on. I also considered Popeye, as I expect in the future she will spend a lot of time chasing after olives. Don't make me explain that one. In the end we decided on '*Pepita*' which basically means 'Pip' in English.

I said last year after working in the olive groves, "First day, last day." It nearly killed me. Well, like going to the dentist, the pain is soon forgotten and as Javier's family and Fernando's have been so good to us, we said we'd do a few days free of charge.

I did the first day with Javier's family, and my job entailed picking up the olives that had fallen from the trees. By the end of the day I couldn't stand up straight. The next day I was to do the same whilst Heather worked with Fernando and Adori, the couple that ran the bar and also have an olive grove. At the end of the day I was almost crippled. Heather greeted me at the door and said, "I don't know what's wrong with you, I thought it was fun."

"What exactly did you do?" I asked.

"We started at 9:30, raked a few olives up, stopped at 11:00 for half an hour for a sandwich and a beer, then I hit the tree to make some fall off until 1pm. Then we stopped for 40 minutes and had some dinner and a chat, and at 2:30 we packed up and went home."

In comparison, I started at 9:00 working on the side of a hill that would make a Ranulph Fiennes expedition look like a stroll along the canal. I had to grip a tree root whilst picking the olives to prevent me from sliding backwards. At 1:30 we stopped for a quick sandwich and then straight back to work until 4pm. "Tomorrow I'm doing a day with your lot," I said.

The next day was a walk in the park. Just like Heather said, the day was punctuated with breaks for meals, drinks, and laughter. I suppose the difference was because Javier's family had over 5,000 trees to get through, while Fernando only had 1600.

The day finished and all Heather's and my work gear was put away for another year...or that's what we thought. Ashlie came up for the weekend and in the bar Adori was relaying the story of our contribution to the local olive economy. "That sounds like great fun," said Ashlie. So that was us pencilled in for another day's work.

The following Monday we all turned up and began grafting. Our main job was to hit the trees with 8ft wooden poles to dislodge the olives. It was then I realised Ashlie, instead of whacking the tree, was tickling each individual olive, hoping they would lose their grip whilst laughing.....pathetic. At the end of the day Adori pointed out that last year I did one day, this year 4 days. Next year we could do it all season and get paid for it. We'll see.

As I promised my mother, we returned to the UK the following month. It was to be Ashlie's birthday and she wanted to celebrate it with all her friends. Once again we had a fantastic time and it was nice to see family again under more pleasurable circumstances.

Whilst in the UK we received a quick lesson on how easy it is to get into debt. When we went to pick up a hire car at the airport, the man at the desk told us the system had changed and he needed our credit card details. Unfortunately we only had debit cards. Fortunately, Ashlie had one and saved the day. Realising this could be a problem in the future, we went to see the manager at Yorkshire Bank.

She invited us into the office and we told her we wanted a credit card. "No problem," she announced and got the form out. "Address?" We paused then gave Heather's mother's. Recognising our hesitation the manager asked. "Is this where you live?"

"No, we live in Spain." The manager frowned and looked down at the next question. "And what is your combined annual income?" Heather and I looked at each other before I replied, "Nothing!" After checking our account on screen and probably finding we didn't hold much in that account, the manager said she would need to speak to somebody and left the office. At this point Stacey and Ash came wandering into the bank. I could see them through a gap in the door and let them in. I explained we might be a while so they asked for the car keys and said they would wait outside for us. As they left the manager's office (that coincidently opened out to the large queue at the tills) I pushed them out and shouted "And pay your bills in time!" before slamming the door. They told us later that the entire bank turned and watched them leave.

Eventually the manager returned and said that our application would be processed but couldn't promise anything. As we left Heather and I agreed that under the circumstances we wouldn't give ourselves a credit card.

The card arrived two weeks later and we have a £10,000 limit. (Memo to self: If our savings runs out, about 20 credit cards should sort it!)

Chapter 21
Whole New World

At the end of the week our last visit was to call and pick up my mother. Now we knew this was going to be quite an experience for her, as the last time she visited a foreign country was in 1942 when she was evacuated to Wales.

On the morning of our departure we called to pick her up and there she was, waiting next to her case. We had already warned her that there is a 15kg limit but I thought I'd double check and asked her for the scales. 20KG! Half an hour later we were back within limits.

During the car journey to the airport, my mother asked "Where exactly are we going?" I knew her memory had been really bad, and was getting worse, so I replied calmly, "the airport."

"No I mean where to?"

I gave Heather and Ashlie a side-glance, "to my house."

Exasperated she continued, "I know that but where is your house?"

"Spain!"

"Oh shit I told everybody I was going to Italy." This was going to be a long 10 days.

At the airport we checked in and waited. Eventually our flight was called through to security. I said to my mother, "As you get to the X-ray machine you need to take your jacket off and put anything and everything in the plastic tray. I mean everything." As we moved forward we all got channelled into different queues.

The alarm attracted everybody's attention, but I must admit I was a little more than surprised when I saw the security officer twanging the front and rear of my mother's bra, before delving into her pockets. Eventually, slightly embarrassed, she was allowed through. "I don't know what caused the machine to go off," she said, tucking her clothes back in. She then pulled a plastic bag of coins from a pocket, "unless it was these." Heather and Ashlie looked at each other. "Or these." She then produced a tin of mints. "Then again I suppose it could have been these." A small bag of jewellery appeared from nowhere.

This is going to be a very, very long 10 days!!

Aboard the plane my mother removed her 'word search' book from her bag and settled down. She wasn't anxious about the flight because although she hadn't been to a different country, she had been up flying with me a few years ago, flying being one of my hobbies. She'd enjoyed it so much she wanted me to take her up again to do aerobatics, but my dad knocked that idea on the head.

It's funny but for some reason, like my father, Heather has never shown much confidence in my capabilities in the air. I have had the flying bug since she bought a 30 minute flying lesson for me as a 30th birthday present. To be truthful it's not just flying with me she doesn't like, she just hates flying in general.

Twice a year Heather just about manages to climb the steps of the holiday company's jet and place her life in the unseen hands of the smart, middle aged professional in the front. For the next few hours she anchors herself to the chair, her hands gripping the arm rest until her knuckles loose their colour, and that's where she stays until the aircraft comes to a full stop at the other end, regardless of any request her bladder may make along the way.

It's unfortunate that Heather has been unable to place in me that same blind trust that she gives the jet pilots. It may have something to do with the thirteen car crashes I had during the first two years that we knew each other. (Only two being my fault, of course.)

One day after a lot of persuasion and a little begging, Heather eventually agreed to a short trip over the local countryside. I think it helped when I reminded her that she had paid half of the thousands of pounds it had cost to acquire my newfound skill. Before she could change her mind I was on the phone and had booked an aircraft. G-B-N-O-E was the call sign of my trusty steed for two one-hour slots the very next day.

The next morning Heather jumped out of bed and ran to the window. How keen, I thought. She drew back the curtains and revealed a clear blue sky and little wind. An instant look of disappointment swept over her face. It was then that I remembered the day before I had agreed to a number of provisos to our trip, one of these being if the weather wasn't perfect, we would cancel.

As the sun peaked, we swept gracefully into the car park at Sherburn Aeroclub, the local airfield. Getting out of the car, a small Cessna flew over our heads at about 100 feet, presumably on finals. Heather instinctively ducked. "What was that?" She stuttered.

"Just an aircraft coming in to land," I said with my newly adopted jet pilot tone.

"We are not going up in one of those little things, are we?" I know size isn't everything but somehow this felt like a personal attack. I forced a smile. "Don't worry, it's big enough to take us to meet the clouds." Heather's head tilted, her eyebrows dipped in the middle and she said in a voice a little deeper than normal. "What do you mean clouds?"

"I was speaking metaphorically, come on." I said taking her arm and leading her into the clubhouse.

After the paperwork was completed and weather checked I escorted my hesitant passenger across the tarmac to our waiting aircraft. We walked between a large twin-engine beast and a formidable looking helicopter. Heather eyed them suspiciously, making sure she was out of reach, as you would sneaking passed a chained scrap yard dog.

I asked her politely to stand by the wing as I began to check the aircraft. Lifting the cowling to check the oil and brake fluid, an enquiring voice asked, "What are you doing?" I knew that she knew I am not very good when it comes to things mechanical. In fact to be honest I don't think I've ever seen my car engine and I have had it nearly a year. Before I could stop myself, out came the flippant reply: "I don't know but everybody lifts this thing up when they walk round the aircraft." Of course I was joking but as I tried to stop the words coming out, she turned and started walking away. "I'm sorry!" I shouted, dragging her back and showing her exactly what I was looking for.

Once in the aircraft we settled ourselves down. Next came the bit I had been dreading; there was no way to avoid it, THE PASSENGER BRIEF. I know this is a necessary evil but that didn't make me feel any better, nor Heather, come to that. As I explained what to do 'if' things go wrong, it just made her face turn. How does the song go? 'A Lighter Shade of Pale.'

Checks and brief complete, I started the engine, or should I say tried to start the engine. Each turn of the key created a large judder, then a cough and a splutter. Being the first to fly the aircraft that day I had anticipated this, but no matter how I tried to explain it away I was on a losing ticket.

One more cough and she was off—the aircraft I mean, not Heather. Armed with taxi information, I began moving away.

"Golf Bravo November Oscar Echo lining up 24 for immediate departure."

I asked Heather if she was ok and comfortable, I accepted her grunt as a yes, swung the aircraft around, straightened, and opened her up.

I glanced down to make sure everything was as it should be— temperatures, pressures, etc.—when Heather let out a short scream. I looked up half expecting to see another aircraft in our path. She then added. "We're going too fast and we're not on the runway." My fault, I had forgotten to point out that all the runways at Sherburn are grass, something the pilots take for granted.

I calmed her down and began the climb out. Having no armrest, Heather insisted on clutching my elbow. I respectfully suggested that she place her hands on her knees, as it was highly likely that I would need my right arm in the not too distant future.

In an effort to take Heather's mind off the actual flying, I began pointing out things of interest. "Just out of your window is York Minster."

"Where?" She replied. As God as my witness (with an exceptional view as we were right over his house) I only tilted the aircraft about 10 degrees. If you ever hear Heather's version you would think I had dived to within 50 feet of the stained glass window, tipped the aircraft 90 degrees, opened the door, and tried to kick her out.

By now I had conceded defeat and admitted to myself that Heather was no Amy Johnson. I commenced a slow, gradual turn to the left to put us on course back to the airfield. "Put the wings back level," Heather demanded. I believed this had now developed into one of those situations where one has to show who is in command. "To return the aircraft to the airfield without turning we would need to circumnavigate the earth. Unfortunately we have neither the charts nor the fuel to succeed, so a slight turn to the left is what I'm going to do."

Ten minutes later and we were on finals for runway 19. As I began the slow descent, Heather leaned forward against her restraints (I'm referring to her seat belts, things hadn't got that bad). "Where are we going to land? All I can see is a scrap metal yard." I must admit the runway was difficult to make out but after my last domineering outburst, a look was all that was required to make her sit back. She did this with a tut and accompanied the gesture by adopting the crash position I'd mentioned in the brief earlier.

After one of the sweetest landings I have ever performed, and a short taxi, we were back in the clubhouse. Somehow I think it may be a very long time before we do it again.

Back to my mother's arrival. At the village we were welcomed by Javier who had been feeding the cats and the dog. The dog is growing like hell and is now getting more spots like a Dalmatian. I'm now convinced it must be a throwback thing. I introduced my mother. Although she is called Lily, for some unexplainable reason we all call her Frill. "*Está es mi Madre, Frill..... eerrr, Lily*," I said.

Javier smiled, kissed her on both cheeks, and said, "*Hola Frillylily.*" Henceforth for the rest of her visit all the locals called her Frillylily.

Having previously had moles removed because of suspected skin cancer, we expected to see my mother under the *parasols* all the time. Wrong! When I asked her if it was wise to sit in the sun for so long, she replied, "You don't think I'm coming all this way and sitting in the shade do you?" I left her to it.

Now I'm not a superstitious, or particularly religious, person but it didn't go unnoticed that our dog was born the same morning that my father had died. In fact it's not something I have thought about for quite a while, but an incident by the pool got me thinking. My mother had disrobed and was lying near the top of the pool on a sun lounger. When I say disrobed I mean she was wearing her swimming costume, sunglasses, and a large floppy hat. Knowing how shy and conservative she is this must have felt slightly uncomfortable for her.

The dog had been entertaining herself with a squeaky toy at the other end of the garden. It looked up and noticed my mother lying there. I could almost hear the cogs going around in its head. Suddenly the dog began running, picking up speed as it ran towards my mother. From about 5 ft away she launched herself and landed on the edge of my mother's sun lounger. As she started to sit up, the dog lunged again, pulled down her top, revealing everything, then continued up her chest and rammed its tongue deep into her left ear. "WHAT THE BLOODY HELL?!" she yelled.

Is there such a thing as reincarnation?

On the 3rd day of my mother's visit, Anne (Heather's sister) and her husband Adey arrived. They were here for a week and had kindly agreed to accompany my mother back to the UK and to her house.

The pool is now warm enough to get in so my mother, a keen swimmer, became the proverbial water baby, but if anybody splashed her or went near the floats she clung to, the look she gave had to be seen to be believed. In fact it transported me back to the age of 5 when she entered the room and found I had been trying to shoot down an annoying fly with a spray can of WD40. Honestly it was my brother's idea.

Both Anne and Adey dislike the water intensely, and for some reason Anne didn't trust me enough to walk past me when I sat near the edge. I've no idea why!

The 2nd morning Heather went on a bike ride with Anne into the *campo* (countryside). A journey that normally takes Heather and I about an hour took them over an hour and a half. Apparently, not long after setting off, Anne went into the ditch at the side of the road. I vaguely remember Heather's mother spending some time in a similar ditch. It must be a family thing.

Sitting outside one of the bars, I suggested to my mother that she might not feel as left out of conversations if she tried using some of the lingo, like *Hola* and *Gracias*.

"That sounds a bit Spanish," she replied. I give up! As the conversation had brought up the language barrier, I took it upon myself to give our guests a quick lesson. "If you want a chicken sandwich you ask for a '*Bocodillo de Pollo*'. Never ask for a '*Bocodillo de Polla*', with an 'A' on the end." Heather let out a knowing chuckle. "Why?" asked Anne.

"Because a '*polla*' is a man's thingy."

Anne thought for a while, turned up her nose, and said, "Uurrr, who serves them?" I really do give up!

The discussion moved on to bingo. I pointed out that this was a weekly thing and my mother asked, "How will we be able to play if it's in Spanish?"

"I'll repeat the numbers called in English for you," I replied.

"But if they are written in Spanish on the card how will we know which is which?" asked Adey.

"They write them the same as the English!" God I'm surrounded by them. I'm beginning to know how General Custer felt.

Bingo night arrived and once again the bar was full. We all got ourselves a table and as each of the locals entered they were formally introduced to Anne, Adey, and Frillylily. Van Cleef joined us and was in his usual mood…I'm black and blue.

Frill was sitting between Heather and Anne when one of the local ladies came in and asked Heather if the other 2 were both her sisters. Heather translated to Anne and my mother. The comparison on their faces was amazing. My mother looked like she wanted to adopt the woman and Anne looked like she wanted to gouge the cows eyes out.

Bingo started and it wasn't long before my mother called. I must admit I was tempted to tell her that she had to shout some obscure Spanish swear word. But remembering Heather's mother's reaction when she eventually found out what '*borracha*' meant, it just wasn't worth it.

My mother, embarrassed, went forward to collect her winnings, about €25 (£17). I jokingly reminded her that we had agreed beforehand that all winnings would be put together to pay the bar bill at the end of the night. For some reason her bad memory seemed to have forgotten this.

On the last night it was warm enough to sit outside the bar and everybody came to see them all off. Halfway through the night one of the young lads arrived on his motorbike. "I wouldn't mind a go on that," Anne said. So off she went clinging onto the back for dear life.

My mother had wanted to take home a bottle of Baileys but we had forgotten to get one in town. When we settled up I asked Fernando if he'd sell me one. The next thing I knew he'd brought one over for her and refused any payment.

The night ended with Adey at one side and me at the other as we helped my mother walk home.

Bright and early the next morning we drove our guest to Granada airport, my mother nursing her first hangover in a very long time. At the airport they all checked in. Remembering our outbound journey, I explained to my mother that as she went through security EVERYTHING went in the plastic tray.

Anne and Adey drifted ahead and through the arched metal detector.

My mother kissed us goodbye, went past the barrier and was given a plastic tray. She just stared at it. "PUT ALL YOUR STUFF IN IT," I shouted, which she did. She slid the tray toward the mini x-ray machine, stopped, and started taking her things out of the tray to put on the small conveyor belt. "NO MOTHER, PUT THE WHOLE TRAY IN!"

Anne turned when she heard me shout, and in fact everybody in the airport did. Alas, she could do nothing as she had already gone through the system. "NO MOTHER, PUT IT ALL THROUGH!" She lifted her jacket from the tray.

"THIS FIRST," She shouted back.

"MOTHER JUST PUT THE FFFFF..... TRAY THROUGH." Eventually she realised what was required, and off she went, without the alarm going off this time.

Chapter 22
All's Well That Ends Well

The cats have at last settled into their new lives in the sun. They spend their days as most cats do, sleeping. It seems the only time they move is when the sun goes round and they in turn have to search out another piece of shade to continue dozing.

Pepita has, how shall I put it… come of age, and is now the focal point for all the male dogs in the village. Not wanting to increase the family anymore, we decided a visit to the local vet was in order. We arrived at the vet's, having rang a couple of days earlier for an appointment. I felt so guilty when the vet injected the anaesthetic into her paw. The dog just looked up at me, sighed heavily, and then went to sleep. Two hours later we went to pick her up. How sorry she looked. The vet said to bring her back in a week for the stitches to be removed and gave us one of those large plastic cones to stop her from playing with her privates.

Back we went to the vet's. He asked us to hold down *Pepita*, so I got the head and Heather the legs. After cutting and removing several of the stitches the vet said, "Did you see how I did that because you have to take out the last 2 in a couple of days."

Mmmm. I'm thinking a discount should have been offered at this point. I didn't realise it was a DIY vet.

A couple of days went by and fortunately an extra pair of hands was available because Javier was visiting. I asked Heather to get the head and Javier to get the legs. Within seconds the dog was kicking out like billyo, just as I had the scalpel poised over her stomach. I then looked across and found out why. In the vet's I had caressed the dogs head and whispered caring thoughts to subdue it. Heather on the other hand was now grinding its head into the dinning room table as if she was in a WWF wrestling championship. No wonder the poor little thing was kicking out, she was trying to beat the count!

Alas, we failed and went back to the vet's. No wonder he wanted me to do it, he'd gone on his holidays. So another week later we returned, adopted our original holding positions, and the stitches were out within seconds. He made it look so easy.

Ashlie and Scott have settled in to their jobs in Marbella and even went out and bought a car. Unfortunately it was Scott that chose it and as he is a 'none driver' I think he may have been guided more by the price than anything else. I suppose the equivalent of £1000 is what you would expect to pay for a car ten years old but the phrase false economy springs to mind.

During the first month they had to take it to the garage because the lights wouldn't work. The mechanic said water had gotten into them. I asked Ashlie if she had been dipping her headlights, but she wasn't amused. A week later the wiper fell off and the radio stopped working.

Another week passed and we received a call from Ashlie explaining how the car had broken down on the motorway. The next day I went with her to the garage to get the verdict. The mechanic explained how on inspection he had found that the engine had no oil or water.

"Did you put any in?" I asked my blank-faced daughter.

"Well a light kept coming on. Me and Scott looked for the dipstick but couldn't find it so we just left it." I suggested if they had looked in the wing mirror, they would have found two dipsticks.

"I thought I heard your mother telling you to carry water in case you broke down."

"Oh, was that for the engine? I put cordial in it. I thought she meant that I might need it."

The bill for repair was to be £2000, so I told her she would be better off letting the garage scrap the car. The garage owner said this wasn't a problem and just needed the documents for the vehicle. Whilst Ashlie retrieved these from the glove compartment I saw through the car window that the handle had come off in her hand. When she returned, I asked, "Who did you buy this car from? A clown, at a circus by any chance?" Glancing down at the number plate, beneath the letters was the name of the garage who had supplied the car when it was new: BUGGER MOTORS - SPAIN. A well placed ED might have been more appropriate.

Driving home I could tell she was a little upset. I told her to forget all about it and just put the whole, sorry episode down to experience. "Sometimes buying cheap costs you more in the long run," I offered as a piece of fatherly advice.

After a couple of minutes of travelling in silence Ashlie turned to face me with a big grin on her face and announced. "Me and Scott saw a house for sale the other day, it was only £15,000 pounds." I sighed, rubbed my eyes and muttered to myself, "Lesson not learnt then!"

Although Ashlie eventually changed jobs and is now working in a nursery in San Pedro, Scott is still at the estate agents they both originally joined. The money he says is very good, but the hours he had to work initially were incredible. He would work 7 days a week, 3 of which would be time spent in the UK. Fortunately, after a few months he transferred to the training department and then on to recruitment. He is now the manager of recruitment and gets to choose which foreign trips he takes.

The other day he got 1-hour notice that he had to give a short talk to over 500 of the company's employees about their moves into the Eastern Block market. He said to me on the phone that he wanted to drop in a few jokes but couldn't think of any. I told him he should have rung me. I then furnished him with a few off the cuff, like, "Soon all the people will be 'Russian' over here to buy property, and some may decide to 'Romania' for good." The sigh on the over end of the phone told me he was glad he didn't bother.

Since Scott moved down to the coast I have begun to miss the games of tennis we used to enjoy. I have, however, found a new partner. I mentioned earlier our friends Jim and Diane. Well, as it turns out, Jim was a goal keeper for Derby County back in the '70s and quite keen on tennis. The fact that he is also 70 years old means I may actually have a chance of winning a game. WRONG! If he hadn't gone into football he could have been a professional tennis player. We play nearly every week and I've never won a game yet. Can you imagine how humiliating that is?!

Meanwhile, Stacey has bought a house in England with one of her (female) friends. I think the idea to come back in a year's time as a missionary has now been put on the back burner, but along with all the young men of the village, we eagerly look forward to her visits, often accompanied by her friends. Things haven't changed. On her last visit she broke the filter in the pool, the bike, again, and…the dog. Yes, every time she plays with *Pepita* she somehow looses a tooth. On these occasions I tend to refer to Stacey as a 'slack mare', in fact I know it was wrong but when frustration got the better of me I would call her that when she was younger—yes she was one then as well.

I recall attending an opening of one of my customer's, and friends and family were also invited. Stacey would have been about 6 years old. As we left I got talking to a man and after another 5 minutes we said our goodbyes. Stacey asked, "Who was that man with the chains around his neck?"

"That is the Mayor." I replied, smiling at the man as he pushed his chest out. Stacey thought for a moment then announced loudly: "SLACK MARE?"

My mother, having fulfilled one of her ambitions to travel abroad, is now settling down to life on her own and is even back at the gym she loves and swimming 60 lengths three times a week—not bad for a seventy-three year old. She's already booked to come and see us again. In fact, I have just received the confirmation from the travel company by e-mail. A new rule introduced by the Spanish authorities means you must submit certain information before you travel. I clicked on the icon and was asked details like date of birth, origin, etc. These were selected with drop down menus. I decided to glance through them, so I would know what details to gather from my mother. I just clicked anything so I could get to the next page, and then clicked on the word 'Next'.

Thank you for your information. This has now been registered.

Oops. Apparently I have just registered my mother as a six-year-old Columbian boy with a false passport. I suppose I had better ring somebody, or it will be more than her bra they will be twanging as she steps through security.

We have been in our new house for just over a year now and I think all the family agrees that the decision we made to up sticks and move lock, stock, and barrel, to pastures new had been the right one

All in all it's all been an adventure I wouldn't have missed for the world.

As I write this Manuel has just finished some work we needed doing near the pool. He leaves and shouts "*Adios*" and I reply with "*Gracias*." He stops, looks over his shoulder, and says "Allaaannnn. Yooo wankerrr!"

I wonder what could have warranted such abuse. I smiled to myself, and then shouted back, "Manuel, it's not, 'Yooo wanker', it's You're welcome!"

26293264R00107

Printed in Great Britain
by Amazon